THE MYST...
SOLOMON'S
RING

THE MYSTERY OF SOLOMON'S RING

AVA & CAROL DETECTIVE AGENCY

THOMAS LOCKHAVEN

TWISTED KEY
publishing
2018

First Printing: 2018

ISBN 978-1-947744-17-2

Twisted Key Publishing, LLC
405 Waltham Street Suite 116
Lexington, MA 02421

www.twistedkeypublishing.com

Ordering Information:
Special discounts are available on quantity purchases by corporations, associations, educators, and others. For details, contact the publisher at the above listed address.

U.S. trade bookstores and wholesalers: Please contact Twisted Key Publishing, LLC by email twistedkeypublishing@gmail.com.

CONTENTS

I
CARB-LOVER'S PARADISE

"I have one question, and one question only," Ava said carefully.

She and her best friend, Carol, sat on the hotel bed with their hands behind their backs, fingers crossed for luck. Out of the corner of her eye, Ava could see Carol biting her lip.

"All right, I'm listening." Beth Clarke, Ava's mom, raised an eyebrow at her daughter.

"Can we…," Ava took a dramatic breath, "order room service?"

Mrs. Clarke leaned back, narrowing her eyes, a smirk pulling at the corner of her mouth. "We have plenty of cereal bars, you know."

Carol elbowed her. "I *told* you!" she whispered. Just moments before, Carol had suggested that they just eat the cereal bars—but Ava had hissed, "*Real food.*"

Ava groaned, rolling her eyes back like she was dying. "But *Mom*, we're in Italy! All we've had is airplane food, and we've been at this hotel for like three whole hours! We *have* to eat spaghetti!"

"Where does it say that?" Ava's mom teased.

"Right here, in Dad's guidebook!" Ava got up to grab the guidebook her dad had packed for them, a thick, clunky book entitled *Pasta Paradise: A Carb-Lover's Guide to the Italian Homeland.* "Hey, at least I didn't ask for a pony."

"Or a unicorn," mumbled Carol.

Ava's mom chuckled and threw up her arms. "Okay! Your dad is currently trekking his way through the Amazon jungle…and he did go to the trouble of getting *that* book for you—I guess you've gotta order room service."

The girls whooped triumphantly and gave each other a high-five.

"Only one meal each—no appetizers—and a dessert to split. Understood?"

"You got it, Mrs. Clarke," Carol said, crossing her heart. "I'll make sure of it."

"I bet you will," she said back, smiling. "Now, when I'm at my meetings, I need you guys to behave! Ava, don't drive the hotel staff crazy. No crazy adventures. No experiments with the microwave…."

"I just wanted to see if it was a quicker way to cook an egg," offered Ava apologetically. "I had no idea they would explode."

"It was epic," smiled Carol, "but, uhm, more of a learning moment," she murmured when she saw Ava's mother arch her eyebrow.

"Lastly," continued Ava's mom, "movies cost money. We don't want a repeat of our stay in New York when you binge-watched every Star Wars movie ever made."

Ava smiled. "I gotcha; Mom...your memory is truly impressive."

"Carol," Beth continued, "you're in charge of making sure the room service doesn't get out of control."

"Okay, Mrs. Clarke, we promise," Carol said, as she bounced over to the menu on the desk with Ava right behind her.

"Can Dad get my texts in the Amazon?" Ava called out. "I want to send him a picture of our first authentic Italian dining experience."

"Yes, when he's back at base camp with the other scientists, he can download your texts. The SIM card that I put in your phone works in over thirty different European countries."

"Impressive," said Ava, jutting out her jaw. "Thank you, Mom. You rock!"

Ava's mom, a journalist, had invited her daughter and Carol to join her on her trip to Italy for a journalism conference. When Ava's mom suggested it, Carol's parents thought it was a great idea to "teach the kids more about the world." Plus, Ava knew Carol's parents were going to be out of town, and Carol would rather hang out with her best friend than stay with her Great-Aunt Marge, who smelled like old cheese and turnips.

So, Mr. and Mrs. Miller bought Carol a ticket, and the three of them flew way across the Atlantic Ocean to Italy to stay in the fanciest and most beautiful hotel Ava had ever seen, the St. Regis in Florence. Ava wasn't sure why, but every time she said the name *St. Regis* she heard a heavenly choir belt out "Ahhhh" and then a little bell chime. She was pretty sure Carol heard it too, but she was too cool to mention it.

Their hotel room was huge, with two humongo beds, one for Ava's mom and one for Ava and Carol, with a view of the Arno River right outside their window.

"I'll be back in a couple of hours," Ava's mom said, dropping a kiss on each of the girls' heads. "Remember, no *big adventures*—and I'm looking at you, Ava." Mrs. Clarke pointed two fingers at her eyes and then one back at Ava.

"Bye, Mom!" Ava said, waving her away. "Love you more than chocolate!"

Carol looked at Ava, shocked. "Really?"

"Okay," laughed Ava, "she's a close second."

As the hotel room door clicked behind Mrs. Clarke, Ava and Carol tackled the menu again.

"Oh my gosh, we should order the pasta primavera, the cheese ravioli, get a marj-hair-ita pizza, and this…whatever this thing is," said Ava, pointing at the dessert page to something that looked layered with cream and chocolate.

"Okay, first off, the word you just destroyed is a margherita pizza, and second off, your mom just said we can't go overboard with the food," Carol explained. "I'm not going to take the fall for your—"

"Orrrr," Ava drew out, interrupting Carol, "we could order everything on the menu and make a castle out of all of the food and live there forever. Maybe that's what a 'carb-lover's paradise' is, like in the guidebook," she snorted. *Adults are so weird.*

"C'mon, let's just pick something and call room service to bring it up. Dibs on *not* having to call them," Carol rushed to say.

Ava thought about arguing about it, but she knew she'd been beaten. "Rats. Fine," she said, sticking out her tongue to Carol's *Hah!* and picking up the phone. "Know what you want?"

They decided on spaghetti with extra meatballs for Ava. Carol wanted something called lasagna casareccia, so Ava had to hand the phone over anyway so Carol could properly pronounce it. Carol said it was easier for people who knew some Spanish to get used to the Italian accent, and they both knew Carol could ace any Spanish quiz. She was pretty much a whiz with languages. They went with the dessert Ava had pointed to, something called tiramisu.

A knock came on the door a half hour later. Carol thanked the room service waiter with an emphatic "*Grazi!*" Ava dug in her pocket and fished out a beautiful shiny quarter. She placed it in the gloved palm of the waiter and winked. He looked from his hand, back to Ava, and then back at his hand—a confused look on his face.

"Oh yeah, sorry! *Grazi!*" smiled Ava as she waved goodbye and shut the door in his face.

The warm smell of marinara sauce filled the room, and Ava breathed it in like she hadn't eaten all day. Carol set the tray down on the floor, where they had laid out towels to make a picnic.

"This looks awesome," Ava said, picking up a shiny silver fork and digging in.

"I was so ready," Carol agreed.

With her mouth full of noodles, Ava picked up the remote. "Let's watch something! I bet you there's a Disney movie or something on here."

"Listening to 'A Whole New World' in Italian would be pretty mind-blowing," her friend said, as Ava flicked through the channels.

But everything was either a boring adult news channel or a ridiculous little kid show. Nothing was in English, anyway. Finally, they settled on dubbed reruns of *Mr. Bean*, and set to work on their dinners. Little by little the food disappeared, the tiramisu (which, it turned out, had coffee in it, of all things) was devoured, and the girls ended up in a food coma, staring blankly at the screen.

"Hey, Carol," said Ava after ten minutes of sprawling on the floor feeling like a zombie. "I'm making an executive decision as the appointed leader of adventurous exploration and declaring that casual exercise is necessary."

"What?" Carol asked, stretching and yawning.

"Oh, come on, it took me, like, five minutes to come up with that," Ava protested.

"To come up with that entire thing?" Carol sounded incredulous. "Really?"

"Do not sass your appointed leader of adventurous exploration!" Ava said, mock-insulted. She nodded to the yellow light coming from their window. "The Arno River is right outside! Let us go walk alongside it."

"You know we can't go anywhere," Carol said, raising an eyebrow. "Your mom's rule. And," said Carol, looking at the window, "it's starting to get dark outside."

"She said that we're not allowed to go crazy with the *adventures*. She never *actually* said that we couldn't leave the hotel."

Carol crossed her arms. "I don't know, Ava. Your mom's been super nice about this trip. I don't really want to make her mad."

"Here, look." Ava reached onto the bed and grabbed a map from her mom's pile of important stuff. She pointed to a red dot.

"This is us, at the St. Regis. Over here…," she dragged her finger an inch to the right, "…is the Arno River. It's right there, next to our hotel. All we have to do is walk across the road and we'll be there."

"That's the Lungarno Amerigo Vespucci highway," Carol pointed out, her long ponytail swaying to the side. "Highway, not a road."

"Carol, you can see it from here!" Ava stood up, dragging Carol to the window. Outside, the city sparkled in the evening, the rooftops of the old buildings pointed to the sky, making their window look more like a painting than a pane of glass. "See it? It's just a small road, with lanes going each direction. It's totally close, and Mom would never get mad. Besides, we'll be back before you can say *ciao*."

"It does look pretty cool," said Carol, thinking. Finally, she flashed Ava a brilliant smile. "All right. I'm down. Let's go."

Ava let out a cheer. "Heck yeah! Let's do it. Grab the room key, Watson, and we'll be on our way."

"How come I'm Watson and you're Sherlock in this scenario?" Carol asked.

"Because I'm the one who makes the dumb suggestions and you're the one who makes sure we don't end up getting killed," Ava said, shrugging.

Carol paused before nodding. "Yeah, that sounds about right."

The two excitedly shoved on their sneakers over their socks, racing each other in tying them. Carol grabbed her dark purple coat with the pretty flower design on the collar and tossed Ava her jean jacket with rhinestones on the front pockets.

"Don't forget your phone!" she called.

"Got it," Ava said back as she quickly slipped her iPhone into her jacket, thanking her lucky stars her mother and father had been kind enough to give Ava her dad's old phone. "Do you have the room key?"

"Yep!" shouted Carol. "We're all set. Let's go!"

Ava shut the hotel room door and the girls headed down the hallway. Here they were, on an adventure, to explore Florence, Italy! As Ava pressed the button for the elevator, she looked up at their reflections on the gleaming ceiling. She imagined them walking out of the St. Regis into the great unknown, crossing the perilous two-lane highway, and hiking across the treacherous sidewalk path to finally arrive at the oceanwide Arno River. What obstacles would they meet on the way? A grumpy doorman who refused to let the two girls out of the hotel, or even her mother marching right through the door, upset that Ava had been a bad influence on Carol? Who knew what lay ahead?

Ava smiled to herself. *This is going to be so cool.*

2
CAPTURED

"Wow!" exclaimed Carol as they left the hotel, the huge crystal-clear glass doors swooshed closed behind them. "It looks even prettier at night!"

"You're right," Ava agreed. It was quiet outside, but the lights from across the river shone brightly, the water acting as a mirror against the city and the night sky. The streetlights were tall and ornate, looking like what Carol thought old-fashioned oil lanterns would look like. Carol inhaled sharply, the fresh air totally different than the hotel's air. It carried the scent of the city: traces of spiced cologne, cigarettes, and freshly made Italian food.

"See?" said Ava, completely obliterating the magical moment. "The river's right there. We'll be totally fine."

"All right, all right," Carol said, groaning good-naturedly.

Ava offered her arm. "M'lady, would you care to join me on a stroll to the other side of the street? A mini-tour of what I like to call the sparkling jewel of Italy—Florence."

Carol giggled and wrinkled her nose. "Why are you talking in a British accent? We're in Italy, you nut."

"I'll catch onto the Italian accent later," Ava said, knocking her shoulder against her friend. Carol took her arm, knocking her back.

"At least the road's deserted," Carol supplied as they looked both ways anyway, just in case. They strode to the river, breaking away from each other at the last second to rush to the cement wall and peer over it. The cool air hit their faces as they watched the river, its dark waters rippling lightly in the breeze. It stretched beyond what they could see and they drank in the sight of it.

"Beautiful," whispered Carol, eyes wide. "This is so cool."

Ava nodded in agreement, looking down into the inky black water of the Arno River. "I wonder if it's filled with sharks…Italian sharks maybe?"

"I'm sure, and probably mermaids—this is the perfect time of the year for mermaid sightings."

Ava laughed with her friend. "What do you think is going on with that guy?" asked Ava, pointing toward a man who was leaning over the railing of a small bridge that connected to the other side of the river.

"Don't know," shrugged Carol. "Maybe he's looking for a mermaid. Or…maybe, he's a mer*man*!"

Ava squinted her eyes. A pale-yellow light washed over the man, making his bald head glow eerily, like a miniature moon. Tiny wisps of white hair danced on his head in the cool breeze.

There was something peculiar about the old man. As he stretched his hand out over the water, a quick succession of light flashed from his outstretched hand. The man hesitated for a few moments and then the series of flashes began again. The man's head swiveled left and right as he took in his surroundings. The girls quickly crouched below the wall.

"Why are we ducking?" whispered Carol.

"I don't know," said Ava, shaking her head. "Maybe because he's acting weird and if he sees us...he might stop whatever he's up to?"

Carol nodded, agreeing. The girls slowly slid upward, their eyes just above the top of the stone wall.

"Ava, look at that!" Carol whispered, pointing at the water.

Ava followed Carol's finger and saw a sleek black vessel approaching in the water, headed toward the bridge. It almost blended in, like it was a part of the Arno River. Small bursts of light, mimicking the same flashes the old man had made, came from the front of the speedboat. Someone was responding to the old man with the same pattern of flashes. He glanced around anxiously again, and the girls dropped again behind the stone wall.

"What the heck is going on?" whispered Ava.

A large, ominous shadow passed over the girls. Ava was about to peek over the wall when Carol grabbed her shoulder, pulling her down beside her, putting a finger to her lips. The girls watched as a sleek black car, headlights off, quietly hissed by.

"Electric," whispered Carol, seeing the confused look in Ava's eyes.

The girls watched as the car stealthily passed by as quiet as a ghost. The old man seemed completely oblivious to the impending doom until its shadow consumed him. The girls gasped as two men leapt from the car.

The two men forcefully seized the old man, and one of the men pulled a black hood over the man's head! Carol grabbed Ava's hand and squeezed it, digging her nails into her palm. The old man screamed angrily, lashing out with his fists and feet with the ferocity of a tiger. But he was no match for the attackers and they pushed and shoved him into the rear of the car.

Ava and Carol stood, paralyzed. Everything seemed to be going in slow motion.

With expert precision, the driver reversed the car, right back onto the Lungarno Amerigo Vespucci highway, heading the opposite way from where it had come. Away from Ava and Carol. Carol couldn't decide if she was more terrified for the old man or relieved that they were going away.

Before she could decide, though, a small pastry truck darted out from a small alley just a little way down the road. The men's sleek car careened to the right to avoid the truck and swung out of the road, slamming the driver's side of the car into a streetlight.

Carol and Ava could see some sort of struggle happening inside the car, and they both let out huffs of relief when the old man kicked at the door. With a bang it flew open, and, without a moment to spare, he rolled out onto the street and got to his feet. The girls could see the driver furiously throwing his shoulder against the car door trying to get out, but the crash had wedged his door shut.

The old man turned to run, then quickly changed his mind.

"Why isn't he running?" whispered Carol anxiously as the girls began scrambling closer, hidden by the shadows in the courtyard.

Ava didn't answer—she was completely focused on the events unfolding in front of them.

The girls watched horrified as the other bad guy began clambering out of the side of the car after the old man. Just as the man gripped the outside of the car's doorframe to crawl out, the old man viciously kicked the door closed. The man howled in pain as the door slammed shut on his hand and the window smashed into his face.

Lost in the heat of the moment, Ava froze. Carol reached up, grabbing Ava's elbow. "Get down—they'll see us!"

The old man's eyes locked with Ava's for a moment, and then he turned and raced away.

"Come on," whispered Ava urgently. "Come on!"

Clinging to the shadows, the girls silently followed the old man across the piazza right next to the St. Regis. They watched as he passed by the famous statue of Hercules strangling the Nemean Lion, and then disappeared into the shadows down a small alley. The girls stole a last look at the kidnappers' car, and then raced off into the darkness after the old man.

A car door slammed behind them as they followed the old man. Carol stole a quick look over her shoulder. She could see one of the men clutching his nose, which seemed to be broken.

Carol grabbed Ava's shoulder. "Uhm, we need to hurry! We've got company!"

The girls ran down the narrow alley, passing banks and touristy shops long since closed for the evening. The girls dropped behind a row of mailboxes—they could hear the clattering of the pursuers' shoes clapping against the stone walkway. They would be here in a matter of seconds.

The old man skidded to a stop in front of a shop with the sign "Libreria Aurora" in large blue letters hanging above it.

"Bookstore," Carol said under her breath, almost inaudibly.

Using his elbow, the old man smashed the glass pane in the door. Ava silently noted to look into the power of the human elbow. They watched as the broken pieces of glass fell to the man's feet. He reached through the opening and twisted his arm to unlock the door. They heard a small tearing sound. He grunted; his jacket had caught on a piece of glass still on the doorframe. He made a quiet grunt of victory and it swung open, as his jacket dislodged. He glanced in the direction of the girls as if he knew they were there, and then he hurried inside the bookstore.

Ava was just about to move closer to the store when Carol grabbed her. "They're here," she whispered. Carol pulled Ava back into the shadows and they flattened their backs against a darkened doorway. Within seconds, the two men rounded the corner and ran down the alleyway, shouting to each other as they looked around. Ava could see streaks of blood on the man's cheeks and chin.

The tallest man, who had been driving the car, pointed to the bookstore's door and the smashed glass that reflected in the moonlight on the ground. He said something in gruff Italian, and the other responded in a deep voice, nodding. The tall man held a small black device in his hand. A bright blue electrical charge flashed, making a crackling noise.

"A taser," gulped Ava.

Carol nodded nervously.

The girls watched as the men rushed into the bookstore. They heard more yelling, but it was hard to distinguish between the voices. Suddenly, dozens of crashing sounds came from inside the store.

With her heart in her throat, Carol winced as she heard a loud *boom*, and then another *CRASH*. There was more yelling in fast Italian, the three men's voices lashing out. There was another crash, this one setting Ava's teeth on edge. Then, a blue flash, a short scream, and finally silence. The silence was somehow scarier than the noises.

One of the men stepped out of the store, his shiny leather shoes too close to the girls for comfort. Carol stared up into his face. His nose, twisted to the side...his eyes dark and evil. The man looked up and down the alley. With his face twisted in pain, he took a phone out of his jacket pocket. The old man's kick had done some damage; his fingers were swollen like sausages, and Carol wondered if they were broken. Using his good hand, he quickly dialed a number, brought the phone to his ear, and spoke something in rapid Italian.

Carol strained to catch some words, but she couldn't understand a thing. No sooner did he hang up on the call, though, did a black car appear at the mouth of the alley. A loud grunt came from inside the shop. The second man, wearing a suit, came out, dragging the old man. His back was slumped and his arms hung limp by his side.

"Aiutami," the man in the suit said to his counterpart, who went to him and took the old man's other arm. His head lolled forward like his bones were made of jelly. *He must be unconscious,*

Ava noticed with worry. They began to heave him back to the car, and Ava lifted her head out of the shadows, trying to see more. Eyes filled with concern, she searched for a sign that he was still alive. *Please let him be okay.*

The man's eyes opened a fraction, and an ember of hope flamed in Ava's chest as his eyes met her. He glanced down to his side, and she followed his gaze. With his hand hidden to his captors, she saw his fingers begin to move. They were tiny movements, but Ava knew enough sign language to understand what he was saying. He spelled the word "S-I-G-N." She balled her hand into a fist and moved it slowly up and down. Yes.

She watched as he quickly moved his fingers. She mouthed the letters as he formed them, committing them to memory.

F-I-N-D L-U-C-A.

With a new sense of urgency, Ava nodded once to the man, his lidded eyes closing, and ducked her head back into the shadows. "Carol," she whispered. "Make sure you get the license plate number of the car!"

The girls remained crouched in the doorway until the car sped off into the night. When they were sure the car was gone, they stood, breathing huge sighs of relief.

"That was so, so, so crazy," Ava breathed.

"You got that right," Carol said, shivering.

They stood in the shadows together, waiting to feel normal again.

3
LUCA

"Okay, I have no idea what just happened, but we need to get back to your mom," Carol said, her voice sounding strained. "We've got to call the police."

"Wait! No! We need to make sure that no one else was in the bookstore. He told me to find Luca," said Ava urgently.

Carol paused. "What do you mean he said find Luca? He never said a word to us."

"Three years of taking sign language classes in summer camp—that's how he told me. He told me to find Luca."

"Are you sure?"

Ava nodded. "I'm sure."

"Okay," Carol reluctantly agreed. "We'll see if anyone else is in there. If not, we go straight to the police."

Ava nodded in agreement and Carol took a big breath, looking down each end of the alley before they walked toward the door. The girls pulled out their phones and flipped on their flashlights.

"Oh, no," Ava said aloud.

The place was a disaster. The yellow walls had marks on them like things had been thrown at them before they had hit the ground. Tons of books lay on the floor, discarded. Tables were overturned, and a scattering of papers was strewn across the store. Bookshelves had fallen on top of each other, and blank computer screens appeared lifeless from being bashed to the ground. It looked like the place had been hit by a hurricane. Carol walked to the front of the store, looking for Luca or anyone else who might have been caught up in the destructive melee.

Suddenly the lights flashed on, and Carol blinked and staggered backward, momentarily blinded.

"Cosa fai?" came a woman's voice, screaming. Carol hurriedly translated it in her head. *What are you doing? "Che cosa hai fatto al mio negozio?"* *What have you done to my store?*

Carol's hands went up and her eyes widened as she tried to find her voice amidst the panic. *"Mi dispiace! Non parlo italiano."* Carol whipped her head around. "Ava?!" she called out desperately. "Where are you?"

Suddenly, a crowd of Italian police officers appeared in the doorway. Two of them were tall enough to dwarf the girls. Ava raced from between two bookshelves to Carol's side. They stood facing two officers and a large, squat Italian woman who looked like she could rip a phonebook in half.

Carol grabbed Ava, pulling her in close, happy to have her friend by her side once again.

"Vandals! Did you do this?" one of the officers asked roughly in English, his accent thick.

"No!" answered Ava. "No!"

"What did you do to my store?!" bellowed the woman as she surveyed the damage, her arms gesturing to the destruction around them. "What did you do to my store?!"

Ava looked around, thinking fast. She knew she had to tell the truth, but she didn't know how much of the truth to tell. *All of it,* came the answer in her mind, but Carol had taken the lead already.

"Ma'am, please believe us. We did not do this to your store. We're tourists visiting Italy with her mom, Mrs. Clarke, who's here for a journalist convention," she said, gesturing to Ava. "We were walking by the Arno River when we saw two men in a black car grab an old man off the bridge."

She told how they had struck a streetlight and how the man had attempted to escape, and had broken into the bookstore to try to hide from the bad guys. The bookshop owner and the police listened intently, nodding during different parts of the story.

When Carol got to the part about how they'd heard crashing inside the bookstore after the men had followed their target, the bookshop owner's face twisted up like she had sucked on a lemon.

She didn't say anything, though, until Carol finished recounting what had happened.

"We were going to run to the hotel to call the police…but we were afraid they may had hurt someone in here," Carol said, gesturing around. "We knew we weren't supposed to…but the way they treated the old man…," Carol's eyes dropped to the floor.

"Bene allora," said the bookshop owner, studying the girls with quizzical eyes. "It is obvious they are just young girls, and not a part of the damage. Look at their clothes—they did not do this."

The girls felt the policemen's eyes scrutinizing them. Slowly, the expression of the officer in charge softened and he nodded, letting out a sigh. "Girls, walk me through the story once again."

"Wait, wait!" insisted the robust storekeeper. "The girl's mother is probably worried to death. Should we not contact her?"

The officer in charge hesitated, then nodded. "Yes, let's do that before their mother calls and reports the girls missing."

The woman grabbed Ava by the hand. "Where are you staying?"

"The Regis," replied Ava.

"And what is your name?"

"Ava. Ava Clarke"

"And your mother's name?"

"Beth…Beth Clarke."

The woman nodded and marched forward through the clutter, finally finding the phone buried underneath an upended table. Ava tensed as she heard the woman's voice speak rapidly in Italian.

Thirty minutes later, the girls sat in the back seat of the police cruiser. They rode in silence all the way back to the hotel, both girls staring out opposite windows. Ava couldn't bring herself to feel bad. She felt like she had done what was right. She replayed the events of the night over and over in her mind: seeing the old man's hand, shakily signing the words...*Find Luca.*

Who was Luca? Was the shop bookstore owner Luca? Did she know Luca? Ava wanted to go back to the bookstore right then and there and look around to see what she could find—she had so many questions.

She slowly turned toward Carol. Ava could tell by the way her head hung that her friend was upset. Mrs. Clarke was like Carol's second mom...and she knew her mom was going to go ballistic when the girls pulled up in a police cruiser.

Ugh, Ava thought, *not just a police cruiser...but a police cruiser on their first night in Italy.*

As they neared the hotel, the girls could see Ava's mom standing outside of the entrance, talking with a security guard. Ava immediately felt a stab of guilt. She didn't want to make her mom worry. Carol felt her throat shrink the moment she saw Mrs. Clarke. It was obvious: the woman was furious.

"Ava! Carol!" Mrs. Clarke shouted when she saw the two approach with the policemen on either side of them. They went to her and she hugged them, a glint of relief amidst the anger still clear in her eyes. She looked between the men and the girls. "What in the world happened?"

"Ma'am, could we have a word with you?" the lead officer asked politely.

"Yes, of course. Girls, I want you to go straight into the lobby, find a couch, and do not move from that spot. I'll be in there in just a minute to talk to you about the meaning of *not going too far.*"

"Okay, Mom," Ava said quietly, shame weighing her down. Carol nodded and they went through the doors. Carol glanced back once, feeling powerless. This was the absolute worst. Not only did they fail to help the mysterious old man, but now Mrs. Clarke was upset too.

Together, they sat on the first couch they found, a gold velvet one with cushions that sunk luxuriously beneath their weight, but not too much. Normally, they'd be talking about how it was, without a doubt, the prettiest couch they'd ever sat on that also happened to be comfortable. But they didn't say a word to each other. Despite the excitement of what had happened, the gravity of the situation had settled onto their shoulders and the events of the night had left them gravely quiet.

Five minutes later, Ava's mom walked in without the policemen. She spotted the girls and went over to them.

"Alrighty then," she said without a smile. "Let's go back to the room."

It was a painfully quiet elevator ride. Not even the pretty reflective ceiling of the elevator distracted them. Carol stood in misery. She hated it when adults were upset with her, and Mrs. Clarke was one of her favorite grown-ups. Ava felt it too, chewing on the inside of her cheek. The food and tiramisu they'd devoured sat like a rock in her stomach.

Finally, they arrived. No sooner did they walk into the hotel room, with the door shutting behind them, did Ava's mom whip around with her hands on her hips, her jaw clenched in anger.

"What in the *world* were you thinking?" she demanded of the girls. "Do you have any idea how dangerous a situation you put yourselves into? And did I not *explicitly* say that I didn't want you to go far?"

"I don't know what *explicitly* means," Ava said quietly, her eyes downcast.

"It means 'out loud,' Ava," Mrs. Clarke replied, still fuming. "It means, I definitely told you to do the exact opposite of what you did. Do you know how scared I was to come back to the room to find your jackets gone, with you nowhere in sight? We're in a different country! I know you're both big on adventures, but this is the kind of adventure that you can't have while it's just me looking out for you. Do I make myself clear, girls?"

"But the old man was in trouble!" blurted Ava. Carol looked at her, eyes saying *what are you doing?!*, but Ava ignored her. "Mom, you have to hear what happened."

Mrs. Clarke settled back, crossing her arms. "Telling me excuses won't make you any less grounded when we get home, young lady."

"*Mom*, this is important!" she implored her. Without waiting another moment, Ava began to describe what had happened. After a while, Carol jumped in too, feeling braver.

"We really just wanted to make sure that the old man was okay," Carol insisted at the end of Ava's retelling, her ponytail bobbing up and down as she nodded vehemently. "We stayed hidden until the bad guys were gone…we just wanted to make sure no one was hurt, and then we were going to go straight to the hotel to call the police."

Mrs. Clarke's eyes flicked back and forth between the girls. Finally, she sighed and hugged them both again, squeezing them tightly. "I'm glad you both are okay," she said, and they hugged her back. Ava sighed. There was no bigger relief than knowing your parents weren't disappointed in you anymore. "And I'm glad you both have such courageous, big hearts. But you have to promise me not to do anything like that again, okay? Call the police. Don't try to fix stuff on your own."

"Okay, Mrs. C."

"Okay, Mom…." Ava's voice lowered. "We really were just worried about that old man…."

Mrs. Clarke drew back, looking tired but no longer angry. "I'm going to take a shower and wash off the worry." She glanced at her watch. "I think it's past time that you guys got ready for bed. When I come out, I want to see you in bed."

Agreeing, the girls went to their suitcases as Ava's mom walked into the bathroom, shutting the door behind her. Ava waited until she heard the shower running before she motioned Carol over.

"What is it?" asked Carol excitedly.

"Remember how we split up when we went in the bookstore?"

"Yeah," nodded Carol. "Of course."

Ava reached into her pocket…and pulled out a tattered envelope.

"Is that…blood?" asked Carol.

"Yeah. He must have cut the heck out of himself because he used a jagged piece of glass from the window like a knife blade."

"What do you mean?" asked Carol, confused.

"When I shut the door, I found the envelope on the back of it, with the glass stabbed through it."

Carol's jaw dropped, and she looked at Ava. "Ouch!"

"Double ouch," said Ava. "Our friend had a really bad evening."

"Well," said Carol hurriedly, "what are you waiting for? Open the envelope!"

Ava carefully opened the envelope, dumping the contents onto the bed. A strangely shaped metal ring and a small piece of paper fell onto the comforter. Carol lifted the ring; the metal was smooth, with deep grooves on each side. The decorative face of the ring looked like it had been sliced in half. The body of the ring had strange symbols etched into it...it looked like Egyptian hieroglyphics. The way the ring was made, Carol guessed there was another matching piece that completed or interlocked with the piece she was holding.

Carol turned the ring over in her hand....

"Okay," smiled Ava. "I can see your brain whirring. What are you thinking?"

"I'm thinking you are missing the second part of this ring. Do you think maybe a piece fell out? Maybe he dropped it in the bookstore?"

"What do you mean?" asked Ava as she took the ring from Carol.

"You see these grooves and the decorative face? It's made to interlock with another ring. You know, like those best friend necklaces that are like half a heart, and when you put them together, they make a whole heart."

"Yeah…I know exactly what you mean…and notice I don't have one," smiled Ava.

"That's because I only give them to my best friends."

"Oh," said Ava. "Funny. Hurtful, but funny."

"Well," said Carol continuing, "I think this ring is like that. I think it locks together with another piece."

"Okay, cool…but honestly, it looks like a cheap piece of jewelry, not worth risking your life for."

"True," nodded Carol. "Maybe this will answer our question." Carol unfolded the piece of paper, and her eyes narrowed. Someone had drawn a strange symbol made up of four lines with a small circle balancing on the left side.

"What does it mean?" Ava whispered to Carol.

"I have no idea," said Carol, studying the symbol. "Any ideas?"

"An ostrich? A stork standing on one leg?"

"It looks more like a constellation or zodiac symbol," said Carol thoughtfully.

Ava whipped out her phone and began typing. "Maybe that's what he meant by 'find Luca,'" she said excitedly. However, after a couple minutes of searching the internet, Ava couldn't find a constellation or a zodiac symbol named Luca.

Carol stared at the symbol, her brain spinning as she tried to make a connection…but she had to admit, she was stumped. She looked at Ava and shook her head. "I have no idea what it means."

"It means," said Ava, smiling, "that we need to pay our favorite Italian bookstore another visit."

"And you think your mom is going to let you simply waltz over there after her lecture tonight?"

"Oh yes, after I convince her how old and delicate the store owner is, and that she has a sick husband, and the store is her livelihood…and that these bad, bad men did so much damage…that without our help….” Ava paused, offering a devious smile.

“That little, old, fragile woman needs us,” nodded Carol in agreement. “So…back to the bookstore?”

“Back to the bookstore,” winked Ava.

4
PANTSING: IT'S A THING!

"Oh, man, Ava," murmured Carol. "I don't know about this."

"Why are you worried? Look at those biceps," said Ava as she poked her friend's arms. "The bad guys would take one look at those bad boys and bolt."

"My biceps look like very tiny, sad, deflated balloons," said Carol, flexing as she walked by a pastry window.

"You need to be more positive," implored Ava. "Is the balloon half full or half empty?"

"I think your brain is half empty."

The girls had spent a wonderful morning with Mrs. Clarke, sitting out on the balcony, eating breakfast—watching Florence come to life. Carol thought it was amazing, like a Broadway production. The trio took turns guessing the occupations of different people as they passed beneath their balcony at the St. Regis. The morning brought tranquility—and renewed hope. To Carol, it seemed as if the events of the night before had been a dream....

A beautiful gondola, shaped like an elf's shoe, passed by. A man dressed in black pants with a blue-and-white-striped shirt expertly navigated the river, using a long paddle. Everything seemed so peaceful—just how she had imagined Italy.

Ava had convinced their mother that the owner of the bookstore could barely walk, much less move…and that there was no one to help her since her husband was sick and frail. She insisted that they help the poor old woman, who was probably at this very moment sitting on the floor, surrounded by piles of books, sobbing.

It took some incredible acting, but Ava was able to convince her mother that only they could help the poor bookstore owner. Mrs. Clarke finally agreed, but she insisted that the girls had to go straight to the store, and then text her immediately when they arrived safely.

They, of course, did not mention their true intentions: find the other half of the ring, and find out if the lady had any connections to anyone named Luca…or if she had any idea how they could find Luca.

As if on cue, Ava and Carol stopped just around the corner of the bookstore, far enough away that they could just peek at the entrance. There were still a few fragments of glass, trapped within the coarse stonework, glimmering in the afternoon sun. From their angle, they couldn't see much else. A kind of nervous air hung between the two friends as they peered into the bookstore. Ava quickly texted her mom, letting her know that they had arrived safely at the bookstore, and that she was the best mom who had ever lived.

Ava glanced over at Carol, who was feverishly biting her lip. "Someday you are going to chew your lip off, and they are going to have to make you a new lip…and just so you know, I am not donating part of my lip for your lip replacement."

Carol turned to face Ava. "Really, that's where you draw the friendship line? We are risking going back to the store and having the owner call the police on us."

"We have to check it out," Ava insisted. "It's the only way to figure out if she knows anything about Luca, and if the second part of the ring is there. As far as your lip is concerned…I have no comment."

Ava slipped her hand into her jacket, feeling the envelope against her fingertips. She was all too aware that such a wild part of this crazy adventure was sitting just in her pocket.

"Why do I always let you talk me into crazy things? Let's go for a walk, at night, in a foreign city…let's chase after crazy kidnappers…," Carol muttered beneath her breath.

"Now is not the time for thought and reasoning!" Ava tsked, swatting her best friend.

A clatter came from inside the bookstore, and a woman's voice speaking angrily in Italian quickly followed. Ava's eyes widened. They noticed the shattered pane in the door had been replaced with cardboard, with the word *Aperto* handwritten on it.

"Ahem," said Carol, grabbing Ava's shoulder. "You know, we could come back later…she seems really focused and…."

Ava rolled her eyes and shrugged her shoulder free. She slowly pushed the door open and stepped inside.

"Che cosa? Chi c'è?" What? Who is there?

They stopped just inside the doorway, looking at each other. Neither said a word until Ava's shoulder bumped Carol's. She shot her friend a look: *Say something.*

"Buongiorno, ma'am. It's us, the two girls from your shop last night," Carol said loudly, but she didn't walk closer for fear that the woman would chuck a book at them. Ava didn't blame her. Strange, angry Italian women were at the top of her list as the scariest people ever, followed by angry Italian kidnappers, then rollerblade aficionados next.

"Ahh, the little girls who were in trouble, hmm?" she said. "Come in. Do not be ghosts in the doorway."

Ava wanted to volunteer that she was not a "little girl," that she was twelve and basically a normal human being at that point, but it was obvious that the bookstore owner had been through a lot and didn't need to be argued with. Ava took a step forward, and without missing a beat, Carol walked with her.

As they came into fuller view of the room, Ava looked around and recognized the bookstore's interior. It looked so different in the daylight. Dusty yellow sunlight lit up the books that still lay strewn across the floor, along with the upturned tables and chairs, broken glass, and spilled objects. Dust that hadn't quite settled floated in the air, particles catching the light. In the center of all of it was the woman, her graying hair tied up in a bun with a red bandana to keep the flyaways back. She had a dirty apron tied around her waist, her floral skirt swaying past her calves.

Obviously, one book this woman was missing from her collection was one on fashion, thought Ava. *Bandanas are so 1980s.*

Carol, however, could clearly see the lines on her face, and she felt another pang of sadness. The woman had made some progress, but for the most part, the place was still a mess.

"Whoa," Carol breathed as she looked around. Ava nodded. It looked worse, actually, since they could see all the damage this time.

"Why you just stand there?" the woman demanded. "I do not have time for visitors who want to watch as I work."

"Mi-mi dispiace," Carol said, stammering. She cleared her throat. "May we help you?"

"Why? You make this mess?" the woman barked. The girls jumped. She looked the pair up and down for a moment. With a dry laugh, she swept an arm across the room. "Terrible. They destroy my shop and do not even have the decency to leave…hmm…what you Americans say? A vacuum?"

Ava giggled. "Because that's the right way to leave a place like this, right? So long as they hand you a dustpan at the end."

She snorted. "If only. Well, I needed some new displays," she said, looking at two smashed tables laying at her feet. "Now these ruffians have given me the opportunity. But if you want to help, start by shelving the books…they're everywhere."

The girls nodded, jumping into action. Carol crouched down, picking up an armful of biographies.

"What are your names again?" asked the woman as she righted a table.

"I'm Ava, and this is Carol," said Ava, gesturing to each of them. "She's the one with the large biceps…. I'm better known for my incredibly high IQ and…"

"Ability to annoy everyone," Carol laughed, interrupting her.

The woman chuckled. "You may call me *Signora* Coppola."

"Buon giorno," offered Ava, curtsying.

"Dear Lord," whispered Carol, shaking her head at Ava. "She's not the queen."

"It's *buongiorno*," corrected *Signora* Coppola. "Treat like one word. And now, books." She fluttered a hand toward the ground.

"Libros," answered Ava proudly, gesturing at the books.

"No," said Carol, smacking the back of Ava's head. "She wants you to *pick up* the books."

Carol looked at Ava, who shrugged and bent down to start gathering books. Every once in a while, Ava would pick up a book to show Carol, who would ooh and try to translate the title. *Signora* Coppola would roll her eyes when they did this, but not in a bad way, Ava thought. She looked like she found the girls funny, which relieved both of them. The last thing they wanted was to upset her.

"I guess this one would stay the same," Carol chuckled as she held up the binding of a *Harry Potter* book.

"Only if you say it right," Ava replied. "Ma'am, how do you pronounce 'Harry Potter' with an Italian accent?"

"Better than if you say it with an American one," answered the woman, and the three of them laughed.

Carol smiled. She liked *Signora* Coppola. Her store had been ransacked, furniture broken, and yet she was humming what Carol imagined was a popular Italian tune. She was happy they were helping her.

Ava returned to the front of the store near the doorway, where she had found the envelope that contained the ring and the symbol. Pretending to be placing books on a lower shelf, she crouched down and began searching the floor for the other half of the ring. The door to the bookstore opened, nearly smacking her in the forehead, and a tall man walked into the store and stood quietly. Carol and *Signora* Coppola didn't appear to notice as they righted a table.

"*Signora* Coppola…may I ask you a question?" asked Carol.

Signora Coppola answered her, but Ava didn't hear. Her eyes were on the newcomer, and she was frozen to the spot. *Oh my God*, she thought. *Oh my God, oh my God, oh my God.*

Carol knew she was putting a lot on the line, but she felt like she could trust *Signora* Coppola. "The man…the old man that was taken from your store last night…he said 'find Luca' as he was being dragged away. Do you know what…?" Carol stopped midsentence, and followed *Signora* Coppola's stare. She felt her throat constrict, her heart threatening to beat right out of her chest.

The man made his way through the room, casually picking up a fallen book and examining it and then placing it on a table.

"*Mi scusi, signore, come posso aiutarla?*" *Signora* Coppola said to the man. *How can I help you?* Carol quickly translated in her head. She looked at the man, her lips squeezed shut to keep her jaw from dropping. She could see Ava by the door; her face wore an expression of frantic disbelief.

Why was he here? Did he have any idea who they were? Slightly, ever so slightly, Carol shook her head once. Ava nodded once in return. Her expression molded, to the best of her ability, into one of normalcy. The two continued to pick up books, though much more stiffly than before. Neither of them could say it out loud, but they both knew it.

The man was one of the kidnappers from the night before!

"Buon pomeriggio," he said, nodding to the woman, an empty smile filling his face. He took out a badge and showed it to the woman, who walked forward to look closer. "My name is Inspector Rossi," he said in Italian. "I am looking into the intrusion and attack that occurred here last night. I was wondering if you found anything that may be of interest, say a wallet…keys…anything…."

As she responded, Carol did everything she could to avoid looking at him. The girls cringed when they heard *Signora* Coppola motion toward the girls and mention their names. Ava looked up sneakily, her eyes hidden by her side bangs. The man was studying the two of them, a suspicious look appearing on his face. Ava looked away, heart thrumming in her chest. She was shaking, and she could only hope it wasn't too noticeable.

"Grazi, signora," he said to the woman. He turned to the girls, dipping his chin and flashing a smile, along with his badge. "How nice *Signora* Coppola has some helpers. She informs me you

two girls were here last night during this…mmm, tragic event." He shook his head, glancing around and making a *tsk-tsk* sound with his tongue. "Truly terrible."

Now that he came closer, Carol could see that his eyebrows were thick and hung over his eyes like drapes, shading them. He had a long, thin nose and a bottom lip that dwarfed his upper lip. He smiled easily but there was something off about the way he did, like he had a hundred secrets and it was so funny that the world didn't know a single one. Carol decided that even if he wasn't a kidnapper, which he totally was, she'd dislike him anyway.

Similarly, next to her, Ava was looking at the man coolly. Carol recognized that expression. If he tried to grab them, punch him in the nose.

His grin widened, and Ava was sure it wasn't just her imagination that it turned eviler the farther it stretched—he resembled a real-life Grinch. He reached into his jacket pocket and pulled out a notebook.

"Hmmm…ah yes, here we are. I simply need to review my fellow officer's notes with you…. So, you two girls were witnesses to the crime?" he asked, his lips formed into a smile but his eyes filled with pure evil. His hand carefully brushed open his jacket so only Ava could see the taser hooked to his belt.

Ava looked at Carol, not sure how to respond. If they didn't play along, he may hurt them or, worse, *Signora* Coppola.

Signora Coppola looked at them quizzically. "He is an inspector, girls." She nodded at them briskly. "Go on, answer him."

"Perhaps the girls would feel more comfortable at the *stazione di polizia*. We could stop and pick up your parents, of course," he said, nodding toward *Signora* Coppola. "Perhaps this would be more agreeable?"

Ava tried to convey the fact that something was wrong to *Signora* Coppola through her eyes, but she simply seemed to think the girls were being disrespectful.

"My parents don't like police stations, or post offices...nothing personal."

He inched closer, and instinctively the two inched away. "This is a very serious crime. I'm quite sure you would like to help us solve it, not only for the poor man who was kidnapped but also for your friend, *Signora* Coppola."

Signora Coppola looked from the girls back to the man...confusion filling her face.

"Look," Rossi said, spreading out his hands. "My partner is outside. Let's say we take a nice ride to the police station." He leaned in uncomfortably close, close enough that they could smell the sourness of old coffee on his breath. Ava wrinkled her nose. Ick. "Perhaps a nice ride will jar your memory."

Ava slowly shook her head at Carol. "I think Ava should call her mom and meet us here. Then we can follow you to the police station. Besides, you need *our* help. We are not the ones that committed the crime. So, we are doing you a favor."

Rossi's smile twisted and became a tight thin line on his face. His eyes narrowed. He was just about to speak when Ava started.

"Besides," said Ava, looking between the "inspector" and her best friend. "I just remembered we haven't had lunch. You may not have *hangry* here in Italy, but back in the States, believe me…it's a real thing."

"What?!" Rossi spun around, facing Ava. "This is maddening," he yelled, jabbing his finger forcefully into her sternum. "You will come with me and you will come with me now!"

"Now wait a minute!" cried out *Signora* Coppola. "They are children! What are you doing?!"

Ava stepped backwards, but her foot caught on a small tower of books. With a cry, she tripped and fell, falling on her butt. She blinked and saw a tattered white envelope on the floor next to her. She gasped. It'd fallen out of her pocket. Right in front of her eyes, almost in slow motion, the ring slipped out of the envelope, rolling on the floor before it stopped. Ava quickly grabbed the ring and paper and shoved them into her pocket. Haphazardly, with electricity pumping through her fingertips, she looked up.

The man's eyes were glued on Ava's pocket. He was basically salivating. Ava blinked and realized with horror he had seen the ring. The way he looked at it was like a shark and a small, defenseless fish. The ring had to have something to do with the kidnappers!

"What have we here?" he inquired, his voice awkwardly high. Completely absorbed, he took a step closer to Ava, his attention riveted. Ava looked beyond his looming figure for a second to see Carol carefully sneaking behind Rossi. "Are you hiding evidence from the crime scene?"

Carol had a plan. It was a daring plan, but since it had worked in last year's sixth grade class where Joey Templeton got three detentions in a row for *pantsing* people, it'd probably work here too, right? Praying to whatever saint was in charge of gravity or fashion, Carol yanked down on Rossi's pants with all her might.

"PANTS!" she shrilled at the top of her lungs, the man's pants pooling at his ankles—with small, cute pigs and strips of bacon dotted all over his boxers.

"Ava, RUN!" shouted Carol. She was right, it was time to go. Stumbling over the books, Ava got to her feet.

"Sorry, *Signora* Coppola!" Carol yelled, racing toward the door. She glanced behind them to see the man struggling to pull up his pants.

Ava slammed both palms into the door, with Carol piling in behind her. The door swung open, crashing into a man with a large bandage on his nose. The impact of the door crushed the cigarette in his mouth and sent him reeling backwards onto the sidewalk. The man grabbed his nose, howling in pain.

The girls leapt over him. Looking back over their shoulders, they could see Rossi fighting to regain control of his pants while *Signora* Coppola beat him with a large book and pushed him out the door.

"Get them, you idiot!" Ava heard Rossi's high-pitched voice shout, even though they were already half a block away. "*Get them!*" he screamed.

5
EXTINGUISHED

"That's Nose Guy," yelled Ava, suddenly realizing whose face she had just slammed the door into.

"Who?" yelled Carol as they raced down the alley, the faces of curious shop owners and tourists were a blur as they passed by.

"The guy last night with the hurt nose. Nose Guy."

"Oh!" Carol's eyes flicked to her peripheral. Behind them she could see the foreboding shadow of the tall man racing like a stick figure behind them, a strange whistling sound coming from him. "He's gaining on us!"

Ava quickly stole a glance over her shoulder. She was surprised sparks weren't flying from his Italian loafers as he chased them down. The man was clearly gaining on them with each stride, his nose whistling like a squeaky toy with each breath.

"Hang in there, we're almost to the hotel," puffed Ava, recognizing the start of the Piazza Ognissanti. Just beyond them was the Arno River, and she could see the back of the St. Regis from where they were. They were so, *so* close.

"We're going to make it," she breathed out sharply. They turned the corner to the front entrance of the St. Regis, bolting as nimbly as they could after making a hairpin turn. The doors swooshed open. Ava and Carol jumped inside, just in time to see Nose Guy attempt to put on the brakes, only to be betrayed by his Italian loafers. He floundered, his arms waving wildly, as he skated right past the doorway, sliding another six feet before coming to an awkward stop.

Had they not been *that* close to being caught by legit kidnappers, Ava would have thrust a huge white card in the air with "9/10" on it for the man's near-perfect execution of the Italian slide. *Whoosh....*

The girls gracelessly ran-walked to the elevators, trying to get as far as they could away from the man without causing a disturbance.

They need not have worried. Visitors lined the check-in area. The two bellhops were busy struggling across the lobby with two massive luggage carts overfilled with expensive luggage, followed by an impeccably dressed man and woman who were mercilessly berating the bellhops.

The girls reached the elevator, and Ava hit the open button about a million times. Carol looked nervously behind them. Thankfully with a *ding*, the door slid open, and the two practically jumped in. Carol hit the ninth-floor button just as the evil, loafer-wearing villain walked through the hotel doors. He immediately spotted the girls.

"Uh, Ava," said Carol.

"On it." Ava punched the door-close button over and over again as the man speed-walked toward the elevator. He reached out with his good hand, and Ava realized with dread that they were about to be caught.

"Ava…," cried Carol, voice strained with panic. "Either the ninth-floor button isn't working or this door won't close."

Ava looked around frantically and saw the fire extinguisher on the wall. Without a second thought, she yanked it from where it was attached and pointed the nozzle toward the kidnapper.

His eyes went crossed as he stared down the hose of the extinguisher. She couldn't believe it. He didn't stop.

"You have no idea what you are doing!" he shouted, less than two yards away, teeth bared.

"I do," she replied, and winced. "I'm getting grounded for a month." Her thumb pressed down and the nozzle went off, spraying puffy white extinguisher spray all over his face, just as he was about to reach them. Ava shouted "Here!" and chucked the fire extinguisher at the man, who shockingly caught it against his chest. The doors closed and Ava fell back against the rear wall of the elevator, releasing a blast of air from her lungs as the elevator shot upward.

Carol stared at Ava, and for a good five seconds, neither of them said a word.

"Nice shot," smiled Carol finally. "He has officially been extinguished."

"Nice one!" laughed Ava. "So, why did you hit the ninth floor? We're on the fifth floor."

"Because," said Carol, jabbing the five button, stopping the elevator as they approached the fifth floor. The elevator *dinged* again and the door slid open, absurdly sooner than it did in the lobby. "I wanted him to enjoy his nine flights of steps. He'll think we are on the ninth floor. Come on!"

The girls sprinted down the hallway to their room, skidding to a stop in front of their door. Ava fumbled for her key card, then she paused.

"A-*vah*," said Carol exasperatedly. "What are you doing? He could be here any second."

"My mom might be in there," she replied pointedly. "Unless you want to explain why we're breathing like a pack of rabid lions were chasing us, we have to fix ourselves up. Aren't you the one who usually reminds us?"

"Yeah, okay." Taking a quick second to calm their breathing and fix their clothes—just in case Ava's mom was already back from the morning meetings—they exhaled together, grinned, and opened the door. "Oh, and by the way, lions are scary enough without them having to be rabid."

"Point taken," acknowledged Ava. "Now move—you're blocking my lighting…. Mom? You here?" Ava paused, listening.

No answer. They pushed the door open wider and walked in. No sign of her at all.

"Ah," breathed Ava. "That's kind of a relief. I know we'll see her later, and I've had my fill of adults for the moment."

"Fair enough." Carol turned and locked their door.

Ava shed her jacket and launched herself onto their bed, bouncing on the springs. "Ughhhh…Italy is exhausting."

Carol turned and looked at the back of Ava's head buried among the pillows. She remembered that when they were little, and whenever they'd watch a movie with a scary or super-awkward part, Ava would bury her head between couch pillows like an ostrich who was afraid. "Hey. You all right?"

"We were just chased from a wrecked bookstore by a creepy Italian villain, right after we stood up against *another* creepy Italian villain," she said, voice muffled by pillows. "I'm fine. I do my best thinking this way—the less oxygen to the brain the better."

"Yeah," sighed Carol. "It's also your best angle…." Ava peaked up from her pillow and grinned.

"Thank you for the compliment. I bet it's moments like these that you wish you could soothe yourself by playing your bassoon."

"It's true, if nothing more than to annoy you," smiled Carol as she wiggled her eyebrows.

"I just feel sorry for *Signora* Coppola. It's bad enough that they destroyed her bookstore, and then to have the nerve to walk in like they owned the place?"

"I like her—she's got sass. She deserved a lot better than that," Carol scoffed.

"And the old man…the ring, Luca, that weird symbol…," continued Ava. "Nothing seems to fit together."

"Oh, I was just asking *Signora* Coppola if she knew Luca…but that's when Rossi ruined things."

"Yeah, it's crazy," said Ava, pushing herself up from the blankets. "Did you see Rossi's face when he saw the ring?"

Carol shook her head. "I was too busy depantsing him."

"That was epic," said Ava, a smile growing on her face. "Absolutely brilliant. I wish you'd seen his boxers."

Carol laughed. "I more wished I'd seen the look on his face when it happened."

"Sheer, obliterated freaking-outness," stated Ava. If anyone back at school had known what Carol had done, she'd be a legend.

"Honestly, I'm just glad he was wearing boxers!" laughed Carol.

"Yeah, me too."

"Can I see the ring?" asked Carol, plopping on the bed in front of Ava and crossing her legs into a pretzel. She settled her hands in her lap, waiting.

Ava scrambled off the bed to snag her jacket off the floor, then jumped back on the bed. As she sat up, the envelope slipped out of her jacket pocket a second time, falling onto the comforter. When Carol gave her a look, Ava sighed, exasperated. "Okay, so my jacket pocket is obviously not the ideal place to keep this thing. From here on out, you are the official ring bearer."

"Excuse me. Why do you think I'm capable of holding onto this crazy super-secret thing?" Carol replied.

"Because I'm sure as heck not, and I trust you more than myself!"

"The Sherlock and Watson duo strikes again," muttered Carol, casting a sidelong glance. Their eyes met, and they burst into giggles.

"Okay, okay," Ava said, though it felt good to laugh after the whole ordeal, "we're a no-nonsense pair right now."

She opened the envelope and handed Carol the ring.

"It is definitely half a ring. It looks like it's bronze," said Carol, turning it over in her fingers. Her eyes squinted and she scooted over to hold it under the bedside lamp. The light glinted off the metal, catching Ava's eye. "But check it out—this is kind of weird. It has a very peculiar pattern on its face. It sort of looks like a—"

"Pentagon?" offered Ava.

"No," said Carol slowly. "A pentagon has five sides." That wasn't quite it. She searched her mind to come up with the right word, and when she found it, she almost wished she hadn't. "A *hexagram*."

"A hexagram?" asked Ava as chills raced up her spine, making the tiny hairs at the back of her neck stand up in attention. "Uhm, big brain, isn't the hexagram the...," she gulped, "devil's symbol? That can't be it."

"Hmm...," was Carol's only response as she twisted the ring under the desk lamp.

"Oh, man," Ava groaned. "No way. Please, please tell me that we don't have a cursed ring. If I start saying *my precious*, or become extremely fond of burlap cloaks and bad hair.... Carol, are we going to have to hunt down a pit of lava to destroy this thing? I didn't even watch all *The Lord of the Rings* movies! We don't even know how this thing ends!"

Ava continued to rant about the bathtub being the safest place during tornadoes and the apocalypse was supposed to happen ages ago until Carol, rolling her eyes, got up and plucked a grape from the tray on the desk. Without wasting another moment, she threw it at Ava with perfect aim, thwacking her in the head.

"Hey!" Ava narrowed her eyes. "You heard my mom earlier: No food fights in the hotel room."

"Ava, quit it!" she said. "Think for a second. Why would they kidnap an old man? Why would bad guys be so desperate to get whatever he had?"

"He had the ring," said Ava matter-of-factly, looking at her friend. "The old man had the ring. And he hid it. They were obviously after the ring."

Carol nodded. "I bet my Klaus Thunemann T-shirt we're supposed to find Luca, and he'll know what to do with the ring, and how to help the old man."

"I'm not going to even ask…because I feel like the truth is sadder than anything I could ever imagine. However, I would like to remind you that bassoon rhymes with buffoon."

"He is a world-famous bassoonist," sniffed Carol as she crossed her arms.

"I rest my case," said Ava, ducking as Carol whipped another grape at her.

6
MICHAEL THE ARCHANGEL

Carol grabbed her tablet from her backpack and web searched "hexagram ring."

Carol sighed. There were hundreds of results, mostly dealing with the occult. "Ava, I don't know how much we're going to find using the power of Google."

Ava crouched to peak over her shoulder. "I'll help. Sometimes four eyes are better than two." After about five pages of scanning results, something caught Ava's eye. "Wait. Click that."

"I don't know if that has anything to do with what we're looking for, Ava," Carol said doubtfully.

"I'm not talking about the kitten playing with yarn on a hexagram," she said. Her index finger pointed at the tablet screen. "That one."

Carol clicked it, and a new page came up. She raised an eyebrow. "*Solomon's ring*. Sounds biblical."

"Maybe Luca is actually Harrison Ford…. Does it say directed by Steven Spielberg?"

Carol shook her head and began to read aloud. "No, listen. God gave King Solomon a ring that had magical powers to control and entrap demons. The ring was made of brass and iron. There were two pieces, and when they were placed together, the wearer would have incredible power over the spirit world. The four jewels gave Solomon power over spirits, animals, wind, and water. The four red jewels signify the power over these four realms.

"The ring is said to be part of Solomon's secret treasure, which many believe today has been moved from hiding place to hiding place across the globe, hidden and protected by an ancient secret society of warrior priests—bound to protect the ring and powerful artifacts from falling into the wrong hands. Many men have died in their attempts to find or steal the treasure."

Ava stared wide-eyed at Carol. "Wait a second. That sounds like our old man. He definitely wouldn't go down without a fight...and he risked his life for that ring." She leaned back and crossed her arms, exhaling slowly. "Do...do you think that the old man was a warrior priest?"

"It's possible, isn't it?" she responded. "Something made him trust you in an instant...so we know he wasn't making rational decisions," smiled Carol. "Think about it.... I mean, I don't believe in all of the magical, fantasy stuff. But, what if it is real? Like in that *Raiders of the Lost Ark* movie? What if this ring actually gave the wearer magical powers?

"I mean, those are grown men…and they are willing to beat and kidnap an old man for something that looks like an old piece of junk jewelry."

"I think we have our answer then," Ava said.

Carol nodded solemnly and met her friend's eyes. "For now, we've got to protect this ring, until we find out what's really going on!"

Mrs. Clarke texted the girls that she would not be back for lunch. Ava desperately wanted to go outside and breathe some fresh air, and go to an outside café, but Carol insisted that it would be much too dangerous…and Ava had to agree this time that Carol was right.

As Carol continued to comb through the internet, looking for information to tie the ring, Luca, and the strange symbol together, Ava ordered a large spaghetti and meatball entrée and a half loaf of bread.

"We need a murder board," said Carol decidedly.

"A what?"

"A murder board. You know, like on the detective shows where they put all of their clues on a board on the wall and then figure out how they all tie together."

"Oh, that would be awesome, but—"

Ava's thought was cut off by a knock at the door. "Wow, that's some really fast room service!"

"Wait," whispered Carol. "Look through the peephole to see who it is."

"Good idea," whispered Ava as she tiptoed to the door. She peered through the small peephole. She could see the top half of a twenty-something-year-old woman with a cute little hat. "It's okay; it's a hotel woman."

Ava opened the door slowly, leaving the chain hooked. "Hello," smiled Ava, looking around the woman for a cart or steaming hot tray of food.

"Madam, a gift has arrived. The woman left it at the front desk and asked that I deliver it personally—uhm, a Miss Ava Clarke."

"Oh." Ava cleared her throat and stared suspiciously at the small gift bag in the woman's hand. "I wasn't expecting anything. Who is it from?"

The young woman glanced down at the bag. "I'm not sure, madam; she said it was important."

Ava paused a moment and unclasped the chain. "Okay, thank you very much," said Ava, accepting the bag from the woman.

"Oh, how thoughtless of me! One moment please," Ava raced across the hotel room and grabbed her purse, retrieving a shiny quarter. "Here you go," she said, smiling broadly as she placed the quarter into the palm of the woman's hand. "Have a wonderful day." Ava abruptly shut the door and turned her attention back to Carol.

"Wow," said Carol, shaking her head. "You truly are out of touch with reality."

Ava ignored her comment, too eager to explore the contents of the mysterious bag. Reaching in, she pulled out a small paper book, held together with a stapled binding. A handwritten note was attached to the cover.

"Who's it from?" Carol asked.

Ava studied the note while shaking her head. "It's from *Signora* Coppola, from the bookstore—and whoa, is her spelling horrible! I can barely read this." She handed the note to Carol. "See what I mean?"

"Oh, she's thanking us for our help," she said, a small smile starting in the corner of her mouth. "She's Italian, Ava. She did her best to write this in English so we can understand it."

"So...," prompted Ava.

"She said she found the book on the night of the robbery and thought that we might have dropped it because it is an old tourist guidebook from a place called La Villa De Cathedral. She also wishes us well...and of course to be careful."

Ava and Carol turned their attention to the book. On the cover was a picture of a beautiful statue of Saint Michael the Archangel, wings arched with robes cascading down from where he stood. His face was solemn, but his eyes drew Ava in, making her study his face. Hmm-ing to herself, she turned the book over. The binding around the spine was falling apart just a bit, as old books do, and based on how soft and yellow with age the pages were, Ava was sure it was a pretty old book.

She was about to dive into the book with Carol when a sharp *knock knock* on their door made the girls jump.

"Room service," a man's voice sang out, trilling the *R*s. The girls had been so excited about getting the package, they'd forgotten about lunch.

Ava walked quietly to the door, leaned forward, and looked through the peephole. The man's face looked long and distorted through the lens. Ava could see the corner of a cart draped in a white cloth as well as a collection of silver serving dishes.

She turned to Carol and gave her the thumbs-up. The man smiled at the girls and quickly backed into the room, pulling his cart with him. Carol thought it was ironic that the man who served the food was exceptionally thin. Ava liked him because of his rebellious tie clip (a monkey with green eyes) and pants that were at least two inches short, showing off mismatched zebra striped and leopard spotted socks.

Asking for permission, the man swiftly cleared the small table in their room, placing the newspaper and Carol's tablet onto the couch like they were priceless jewels worth millions of dollars.

Ava and Carol oohed and ahhed as he stepped back from the table. Each girl had a heaping plate of spaghetti, with two meatballs and freshly ground parmesan cheese in a small glass bowl. With the waiter in attendance throughout their meal, they each had a salad, a bowl with olive oil and herbs, two pieces of Italian bread, and a glass of Pellegrino sparkling water. In the center of the table, he had placed a small white vase, filled with a bouquet of colorful flowers.

Ava clapped…completely overwhelmed by the artistry, and for the first time in her life, she reached into her purse and gave the man *two* shiny quarters.

The man left, wondering if it had been his presentation or the socks that resulted in the tiny tip.

Ava closed her eyes, breathing in the delectable cacophony of flavors. She looked up at Carol, who was busy doing something on her tablet. "How can you possibly be on your tablet at a time like this?"

Suddenly, Ava felt her phone buzz in her back pocket. She grabbed her phone, thinking it would most likely be her mother. Instead, it was a text from Carol: *You have been gifted "Tipping for Dummies" from Carol Miller.*

"Funny. Quarters are not a joke! People appreciate the weighty feeling of a nice shiny coin in their pocket."

"Mm-hmm…," said Carol as she grabbed the book and began casually flipping through the pages, not really expecting to find anything. "This book is really old," she said, dipping her bread into an olive oil and fresh herb mix.

She checked inside the cover to see if anyone had written their name or any notes, but she didn't find anything. The book was text-heavy with some photos, but something made Carol suddenly inhale sharply.

"Ava, look." Her finger traced across the soft, worn paper until it reached a small symbol printed at the middle of the page. Under it was a small block of text. Carol couldn't make out all of the words, but she could understand *simbolo di San Michele.* "Symbol of Saint Michael," she whispered.

She pointed excitedly to the picture on the next page of the sculpture.

"Ava," she started. "Ava, oh my gosh. I think we may have just found Luca."

"Wait, what?" exclaimed Ava. "What do you mean?!"

"Look," said Carol, tapping a small block of text. Ava leaned in closer. Beneath the sculpture were the words "Villa De Cathedral, Michele Arcangelo, 1465. By Luca Delia Robbia."

"The sculptor's name is Luca!" said Carol excitedly.

"Only one problem," said Ava, shaking her head. "He's probably dead by now."

Carol closed her eyes for a moment and exhaled. "Of course he's dead—he would be like six hundred years old. When the old man said 'find Luca,' maybe this is what he meant. The symbol that we found is for Michael the Archangel, the artist Luca…," she paused while she read his name, "Robbia created the sculpture…all of these things can't be coincidental."

Ava flattened out the book on the table. "There is something written in the margin." She pulled the page out flat. Scrawled into the margin of the page were the words *"sblocca lo scroll."*

"Okay," said Ava, tilting her head. "Any idea what *sblocca lo scroll* means?"

"Well, obviously it has something to do with a scroll. Give me a second." Carol grabbed her tablet and searched the word *sblocca*. "Ah," she said, nodding. "It comes from *sbloccare*, and it means to unlock!"

"So, unlock," whispered Ava enthusiastically. "Unlock the scroll! Uhm, Carol…which scroll are they talking about?"

Carol held the book close, squinting one eye. The book was old and the pictures gray and faded, but she could just make out what looked like a scroll in Saint Michael's left hand. "It looks like Saint Michael is either holding a scroll or a paper towel holder."

Ava grabbed the book from Carol and examined the picture. "Or one of those big pepper shakers that they have at fancy restaurants. I'm going with scroll, though. One problem: How do we find this statue? We're in Italy; everywhere you look there's a statue. They even have statues of statues," moaned Ava.

"The Villa de Cathedral. The statue is located at the Villa de Cathedral."

"We—" Ava's phone jumped to life, gyrating across the table. "One sec," said Ava, holding up a finger to Carol. "It's my mom." Carol busied herself on her tablet looking for the best route to take from the hotel to the Villa de Cathedral. Thankfully, the cathedral was only a few blocks from the hotel, and the street was lined with dozens of small stores, which meant lots of people and hopefully safety.

"Mom's on her way," said Ava, placing her phone on the table. "She warned us to stay in the room. She said that a conference attendee said that there had been a crazy man in the hotel lobby earlier, wielding a fire extinguisher."

Carol snorted. "He sounds dangerous. I think your mom's right…we'd better stay put."

"I'm sure everything will be okay," winked Ava. "I hear Inspector Rossi is on the case!"

"Oh," laughed Carol. "In that case, I just have one thing to say. Pants!!!"

7
VILLA DE CATHEDRAL

Smack! Ava awoke the next morning to a kiss on the forehead from her mom. "You're leaving already?" said Ava, stretching and yawning simultaneously. "We've hardly spent any time together."

Ava's mom smiled at Ava as she brushed her hair gently from her face. "I promise to make it an early day today. We'll go sightseeing and have a fancy dinner together this evening, I promise."

"And...Mom?"

"Yes," said Beth, looking into Ava's eyes lovingly. Was her daughter about to say something endearing?!

"I would like to report a robbery...and I know who the thief is."

"What?" asked her mom, worry now filling her face.

"I want to report the theft of that dress you are wearing, because I'm stealing it when we get back to the States. Mom, you look beautiful."

"Ava, Ava, Ava," laughed her mom, relief filling her face. "I'll see you this afternoon."

"Okay," smiled Ava. "Love you, Mom."

"Love you too," said Mrs. Clarke softly.

The door clicked behind her, and Ava stared up at the ceiling, a smile plastered across her face. She had the coolest mom ever.

***

The girls hesitated as they exited through the hotel's sliding glass doors. Their heads swiveled back and forth, searching for anyone suspicious. Florence had come to life. The tourists were easy to spot with their maps and phones out, looking confused. Locals worked their way around them, muttering their annoyance in Italian. Bicycles, cars, and colorful Vespa scooters zoomed by on the Lungarno Amerigo Vespucci highway. The sunlight, sparkling like a thousand diamonds, danced across the Arno River, creating a perfect backdrop.

Ava closed her eyes and smiled. Carol laughed to herself: The controlled chaos probably matched what went on in Ava's brain, every second of every day.

After what seemed like an entire two minutes of searching for bad guys, the girls decided that the coast was clear. Carol had mapped out a simple route to get to the Villa de Cathedral on her phone. As they threaded their way through numerous small shops, Ava used the reflections of the glass storefronts to make sure they weren't being followed. Having skipped breakfast, the duo darted into Luigi's Bakery and purchased freshly baked cinnamon raisin bagels coated with to-die-for cream cheese.

Ava thought the bagel was the most delicious thing she had ever tasted in her life. Carol thought the cream cheese must have been made in heaven and sent to Luigi's by angels each morning.

"There's the Villa de Cathedral," said Carol excitedly—gesturing toward a colossal stone building that looked more like a castle.

The Villa de Cathedral was a beautiful piece of architecture with nine majestic towers reaching toward the heavens. Ominous windows reached upward through pointed architecture. *Flying buttresses*, recalled Carol from their art class. At the top of the largest tower, a winged angel stood, raising a sword skyward. Above the archway was a massive balcony containing dozens of sculptures of saintly men. Carol stared at the arched ceiling as they stepped through the doorway. It seemed to pierce the sky.

Ava started walking first, heading to the heavy-looking doors. They were heavy, sure enough, and Ava had to really use her strength to pull open one of the doors, gripping onto the iron and heaving. They walked into the spacious opening, every wall holding an ornate sculpture built into the architecture. The cathedral was filled with golden light that glinted off the polished pews and marble statues, and it smelled of incense, smoky spice, and old wood.

"These cathedrals are more like works of art than buildings," said Carol to Ava.

She nodded. "It's incredible," said Ava, taking in the view.

It looked like something out of a fairytale, where the hero stumbles upon an abandoned castle hidden in the mountains, ancient and beautiful.

"Oh, man," Ava murmured. "This is beautiful. But it's going to be super hard to find that sculpture."

Carol shook her head. "It's Michael. He's important, so they'd probably put him in a place of importance. Like…," she pointed to a statue behind the sanctuary, "there."

Ava looked at Carol, eyebrows raised. "Remind me never to challenge you in a game of I Spy."

"You wouldn't stand a chance," laughed Carol as she bumped Ava's shoulder.

The girls walked through the cathedral up to the statue, which towered over them. Carol couldn't believe it was just a statue. The waves in the Archangel's robes looked so real, and he was every bit as beautiful and intimidating as she imagined an angel would be in person. In one hand he held a spear and in the other hand a scroll. The girls surreptitiously examined the statue, each walking around, looking at the Latin script written below him to the top of his sculpted head.

"Carol," said Ava. "What exactly did that writing say in the margin of the book?"

"Unlock the scroll," she replied quietly.

Ava glanced around, trying not to look suspicious while scrutinizing the statue. "How exactly do you unlock a scroll?"

"I have no idea," said Carol. "It looks like it's a solid piece of marble." She looked around wearily. "There are security cameras everywhere, Aves…we don't want to draw a lot of attention."

"Right, we need to act like tourists," nodded Ava. "I'll stand in front of the statue. Act like you're taking pics of me from different angles, but focus on the scroll."

"Perfect!" agreed Carol as she reached for her phone.

Ava stood in front of the statue, striking touristy poses, while Carol zoomed in on the scroll.

"I got some great pictures, Aves. Your parents are going to love these," smiled Carol.

"Oh, I bet they will. Mind if I scroll through them?" smiled Ava, playing along. "Get it, *scroll* through them?"

"Next time you are alone with your thoughts," said Carol through gritted teeth, "please take a moment and Google the word *subtle*."

The girls huddled around Carol's phone, but, try as they might, they didn't see anything that looked like an opening for a key.

"Maybe there's a button, or you have to twist it?" suggested Ava.

Carol magnified the picture even more. A series of symbols encircled the top and bottom of the scroll, but other than that, there were no other markings on the scroll.

"I wish I read old symbols...."

"Yeah, I don't recognize...," Carol stopped. "Okay, I do recognize one symbol, except it's upside down."

Carol dragged her finger across the screen, centering the image.

"That's the symbol for Michael!" Ava whispered excitedly. "The same one on the paper! Except...it's upside down."

Carol nodded and continued to stare at the image.

"Why would it be upside down?" inquired Ava. "I mean, certainly if Luca sculpted Michael he would...," Ava watched in horror as Carol suddenly climbed up on the base of the statue. "Carol! You can't touch a crazy old statue!"

Using her fingernail, Carol placed it on the edge of the upside-down symbol...and pulled. The marble symbol snapped off into Carol's hand. A small hole appeared. Carol's heart was pounding, adrenaline rushing through her body.

"Carol! Get down—people are looking!" Ava's head spun from side to side. "We are *so* going to jail! Get down!"

"Ava, chill! I found something!" The hole was tiny, the size of a matchhead. And from the hole, a tiny piece of knotted thread protruded.

Ava heard the squawk of a walkie-talkie in the distance. A security guard appeared from a hidden door across the sanctuary. "*Carol*...we have company!" hissed Ava.

Carol set her jaw and gave the string a gentle tug. There was a soft mechanical click, and then, from out of the base of the statue, a thin, small, copper cylinder rolled out onto the floor.

"What in the absolute heck...," whispered Ava, as she quickly reached down and snatched the copper tube off the floor.

Carol jumped down from the statue. The security guard was running toward them.

"Carol!"

"I know!" she cried out. "Run!"

"Stop!" yelled the guard.

Ava and Carol weren't about to stop. They raced through the cathedral, pushing their way through stunned tourists. They burst through the sanctuary into the cathedral's rotunda. They could see the massive doors that would lead to freedom. But just as they put on a burst of speed, a huge guard stepped in front of the door, his legs spread wide, his huge, beefy arms crossed defiantly across his chest. A grin crossed his face as if to say, *Come on, try me!*

Carol was about to shout to Ava that they needed to find another way out when the door opened behind the guard. Ava saw their chance! "High-low!" she screamed. Ava dove headfirst, sliding along the slick marble floor through the beefy guard's legs. Simultaneously, Carol ran at the man at breakneck speed. At the last moment, Ava kicked out at the back of the man's knees, sending him sprawling onto the floor as Carol hurdled him and continued through the doorway.

The girls ran down the steps and down the street, looking back only when the cathedral was a tiny dot behind them. Winded, the girls sat down on the grass, under a small grove of trees, fighting to catch their breath.

"High-five for the high-low!" wheezed Carol.

"That was crazy," gasped Ava. "I cannot believe you climbed up on that statue."

"It's the quiet ones you always have to be afraid of," smiled Carol creepily.

"Well, it was brilliant," praised Ava. She was about to pull out the small copper tube when Carol put her hand on her arm.

"Probably not the best idea to do that here."

Ava looked around. "Yeah, you're right. Let's get back to the hotel."

8
DON'T MESS WITH NUNS

The girls began their journey back to the hotel, both glancing around every now and then to make sure they weren't being followed.

"Ava, stop and tie your shoe," whispered Carol suddenly.

"What?"

"Stop and tie your shoe. I need to see something."

Ava immediately understood; she knelt down and began retying her shoe. "What is it?" she asked as she double knotted the laces.

"They're getting smarter...."

"Who is getting smarter?" said Ava, standing.

"The bad guys. Don't turn around, but there is a man in a suit, wearing sneakers—he's been following us since we passed the bus stop."

"Oh, great...and he's wearing sneakers? With a suit? I hope they're at least stylish."

The girls picked up their pace, maneuvering through the crowds of tourists and locals—catching sight of him on the huge glass windows as they passed each store.

"In here!"

Carol grabbed Ava's arm and they ducked into a busy ice cream parlor. They weaved and dodged through a crowd of patrons enjoying their ice cream and gelato. "*Scusami*," said Carol over and over again. She heard Ava saying it too, but they didn't stop for a second. They continued to work their way to the back of the store, as far away from the entrance as possible.

They reached the back of the ice cream store and turned toward the rear door. The hairs on Ava's neck stood straight up as the man in the suit calmly maneuvered through the parlor with the grace of a shark. Ava could see a swirl of tattoos starting from his jaw and disappearing into the collar of his shirt. His hair was buzzed short, revealing a nasty purple scar that ran the entire width of his forehead.

If he had two bolts on each side of his head, he would look like Frankenstein, thought Ava.

Ava poked Carol, who looked at her friend with a panicked expression. She nodded to the counter, where a girl with a freckly, bored face and hair twisted in a bun, took a couple's money and handed them change.

"Come on," said Carol urgently. "Follow me!"

Ava followed Carol as she crawled through a sea of legs and feet toward the counter, their sneakers skimming the ground quickly. Shouting "*scusa*" to the girl behind the counter, Ava and

Carol leapt over the counter and burst through a door into a kitchen, where young men and women were busy scooping ice cream and making homemade cones. The girls raced through the kitchen shouting apologies and pushed through a screen door. Looking left and right, Carol chose left and the two began running as fast as they could.

Moments later, Ava heard the door slam behind them. She risked a glance over her shoulder. The man was already racing toward them.

"Here he comes!" yelled Ava.

The girls had almost made it to the end of the alley, where they heard the hissing of brakes as a bus pulled into a bus stop.

"The bus!" shouted Carol.

Just a few more steps! The girls glanced back over their shoulders, which was a horrible mistake. Ava felt a jolting impact against her chest. Carol's legs smashed into something, sending her airborne. There was a flurry of black robes and a sickening clatter.

For a split second, Carol thought they'd run right into a second bad guy. That was…until she saw a black and white habit fly into the air. Ava and Carol had slammed into a nun riding a shiny red bicycle, knocking her off her bike.

"*Mamma mia!*" exclaimed the woman, haphazardly brushing off her robe and regaining her habit and straightening the large cross that hung around her neck. She glowered at the girls with all the wrath of God.

"*Scusa*," said Carol desperately. She then pointed at the man in the close distance, running after them. She searched for the words in her head, wishing she'd had a dictionary on her. "Uhm, *male!* Aiuto*. Uhm…hm." She stumbled over her words. "*P-per favore, signora. Aiuto.*"

The nun looked at the man and then back at the girls. She nodded, understanding dawning on her face. *This man is chasing two children! How dare he?!* She lifted her shiny red bike, blocking the alley.

"*Correre!*" she yelled at the girls. *Run!* The girls didn't hesitate—they took off to the right down another alleyway, throwing "thank yous" back to the nun as they sprinted away.

Neither could help but look back. They saw the nun whip back her robe, a picture of absurd drama, and from her belt hung a huge wooden paddle. Something visceral happened to the man, a change crossing over his face. He skidded on his heels, eyes dropping to the paddle like it was made of barbed wire. The nun smoothly and swiftly drew it from her belt like St. Michael slaying his dragon and raised it above her head, the glare she'd given the girls earlier now intensified. As the man attempted to stop his momentum—shouting challengingly, "No! *No!*"—the nun swung the paddle, thwacking the man's head.

THWACK.

Both of the girls winced. *Oooh, that had to hurt.* It worked, though, and he turned and began racing back up the alleyway, the nun coming after him, a flurry of black robes whipping around her, her tongue spitting fire. The girls grinned at each other.

"*Mamma Mia!*" laughed Carol.

"I think that nun's my new role model," said Ava.

"Next stop, the hotel?" Carol puffed as they ran.

Ava nodded. "So long as we make it there alive."

9
NEVER UNDERESTIMATE A QUARTER

The girls raced up the Piazza Ognissanti, the gray stones beneath them practically rumbling as they left small earthquakes in their wake. The wind picked up, and Ava's hair whipped around her face, twisting the strands and making them rough. She had a strange feeling of déjà vu and realized, around twenty-four hours beforehand, they were being chased through the same piazza, by the same kind of people. *Oh, man!*

"Remind me," puffed Ava, "to tell you about a training idea for our track team. It involves dangerous and angry criminals."

"I think I already know what you have in mind," laughed Carol.

"Do you think they were in the cathedral? Or do you think they just spotted us leaving?"

"I think they were watching us," said Carol as the girls slowed to a walk as they approached their hotel. "I think they followed us to the cathedral, but they didn't approach us because they wanted to see what we were up to."

"Oh," nodded Ava, "like they thought that we might know something…and when they saw us with the statue…."

"And the copper tube…they came after us."

As the girls turned the corner toward the hotel's entrance, Carol grabbed Ava's arm.

"Not again…," moaned Ava.

Sitting on a bench was a man smoking, dressed in a perfectly tailored suit. He had a hat on top of his shiny, greased hair, and a cigarette that dangled from his lips like a bird with a worm. They watched him touch his ear and then nod to no one they could see.

"He's here for us," muttered Ava. "He has to be watching to see if we come back to the hotel. And he looks like the others." She rolled her eyes. "It's like those first two kidnappers just kept giving birth to more and more bad guys."

"We have to find another way inside, and I don't think we can use any fire extinguisher tricks this time around."

"I could use it to put out his cigarette," winked Ava. "Don't these guys know it's bad for their health?"

"Come on," nudged Carol. "There's gotta be an entrance in the back."

As they circled around, Ava could see a large truck parked at the delivery bay. The smell of bread wafted their way, and the two inhaled together, breathing in deep. It smelled delicious.

"Okay, I think we could get into the hotel if we use their help," Ava said, pointing at the truck.

The girls crept closer to the truck, watching as two workers transferred bread into the hotel via a huge metal ramp. Each box of freshly baked bread was heaved up and placed on a hand pallet truck, which a worker then rolled up the ramp through a doorway.

Carol caught on and quickly stepped onto the ramp after the last worker headed through the doorway. Ava followed her, looking warily behind them as she went.

The room was filled with barrels of olive oil stacked against the right wall, linens on a set of shelves, and other hotel supplies organized around the room.

"If we weren't being chased, I could literally eat this room," Carol whispered.

Ava watched as the deliverymen ducked through a makeshift door that looked a lot like a heavy leather drape with a plastic rectangular window. The girls crouched next to each other behind several barrels of olive oil, waiting for the delivery drivers to leave. A couple of minutes later, they heard voices, and then one by one, the drivers pushed their hand trucks through the door and down the ramps.

Carol peered through the window and gave Ava a thumbs-up.

"One more second," Carol whispered. Ava nodded.

From where she could peek over the barrel, she saw one of the men walk to the delivery truck, waving at another worker and shouting something friendly in Italian. The man shouted back, laughing with ease. The third waved goodbye as the remaining workers went down the ramp. The girls could see him push a button on the wall. A metal door, which looked a lot like Carol's parents' garage door, began sliding down on the back of the truck, closing off its opening. The last man, satisfied, walked through the room and then exited through the hanging leather door, the sound of his heavy boots disappearing with him.

"That took forever," said Ava, peeking her head farther up. "Think it's clear?"

"I think so," said Carol, standing up. "Whatever's through that door will probably get us into the hotel."

The girls moved cautiously through the door. To their right was a hallway, with a dark blue arrow painted on the wall that said *Cucina*.

"Kitchen," said Carol aloud.

"Sounds like the best way to sneak back into the hotel," whispered Ava.

The girls walked down the hall until they reached the double doors marked *Cucina*. Ava pushed through and was instantly affronted with a mixture of people yelling and scurrying about. People dressed in chef uniforms with tall mushroom-shaped hats on their heads handed each other pots and pans, and orders were shouted left and right. It was an organized mess of chaos, with full meals appearing on plates like magic as they were passed to the back of the busy room.

A woman who looked to be in her mid-thirties with pale blond hair and light green eyes was brusquely walking to her station when she spotted the girls. She stopped, her hawk gaze studying the two, flicking between one and the other.

"American?" she inquired, putting her hands on her hips.

"How did you know?" asked Ava.

"Because you are staring at my staff like they are aliens, and you are not supposed to be in here. What are you doing?" she asked, severe annoyance clear in her eyes.

"We're lost," volunteered Carol.

Ava nodded. "We don't know how we got here. Could you tell us how we could get back to the lobby?"

The woman sputtered. "*Ragazze sciocche!*" She pointed a finger to a bright red exit sign, far on the other side of the kitchen. "Get out of here, immediately! We do not have time for your little games."

In a flash, Ava recalled how terrifying Mrs. Coppola had been the night they first met her. This woman reminded her of Mrs. Coppola too well. *Maybe her daughter?*

Without a second to lose, the girls scrambled through the kitchen, rushing around the chefs and different stations to get to the exit sign. As they pushed through the door, they immediately faced another pair of double doors; these appeared more ornate with a small window built into the door. Carol went on her tiptoes to look through.

"These go to the lobby," Carol stated. She looked back at Ava. "Take a look."

Ava got on her tiptoes. Within seconds, though, she groaned. "We're still in trouble. Rossi's sitting on the middle couch, pretending to read a newspaper! See him…? What's with these guys and newspapers? Haven't they heard of the internet?"

Carol shrugged and gave an *I have no idea* expression. "So, what do we do? We can't go back through the kitchen."

Ava smudged her face against the window, looking left and right across the hotel lobby. "We have to get to the stairs."

"How are we supposed to get to the stairs with that guy sitting there?"

Ava pointed. "There! We could use that."

Carol squeezed in beside Ava and looked through the window. Her eyes followed the direction of Ava's finger. There was a huge cart half-filled with luggage parked about ten feet away. Carol glanced at Ava. "The luggage cart?"

Ava nodded. "Yes, single-file, and our first stop is that giant fake plant. We can hide behind that and then when we're sure the coast is clear, jet over to the cart." Ava paused momentarily. "Want to go first or should I?"

"Are you sure this is a good idea? I mean…."

"You climbed on top of an ancient statue in a cathedral…."

"Point taken," agreed Carol, "but you go first."

Ava pushed the door open slightly, just enough for the two to slip through. She immediately dropped to the floor and began army crawling to the plant.

"Why not just leap out the door and do a cartwheel and a bunch of ninja rolls?!" hissed Carol when they were safely behind the plant.

"What do you mean?" asked Ava, mystified by Carol's remark.

"Don't you think if anyone had seen us, it would have been much more suspicious to see two kids laying on their bellies, slithering across the floor like human snakes and hiding behind a plant?"

"Ah, but that's why you're Watson and I'm Sherlock. You think with intellect and reasoning; I think with my gut. Plus, you proved my point; no one saw us. So my plan worked."

Carol shook her head and moaned. "We'll have a conversation about reality later."

Ava ignored Carol's last comment. She carefully poked a finger through the leaves of the plant, slowly parting them so she could see Rossi.

"I have a plan to distract him," whispered Ava. She reached in her jeans pocket and pulled out a quarter. *If I could just hurl this far enough for it to make a loud noise, we could take off in the other direction while he's distracted.*

"If you're going to distract him, try to aim for the wall closest to his head," volunteered Carol. Ava nodded. "Good idea."

Ava breathed in and out, focusing her concentration. When she was sure Rossi was looking away, she stood and whipped the quarter toward him. She watched as the quarter flew through the air…and then with a *thwack* smacked him on the side of the head.

Oh God, oh God, oh God! Ava dropped quickly to the ground behind the plant.

"Hey!" yelled Rossi sharply, jumping to his feet, looking around the lobby.

Carol looked at Ava in disbelief. "I thought you were going to distract him, not hit him in the head!" she yelled-whispered.

The man circled around the couch before looking up at the ceiling and rubbing his head. He looked back down and paused. Bending, he picked up the quarter and held it in front of his face, turning it over carefully. An American quarter—Montana on one side, an eagle on the other.

He touched his ear, and the man outside stood up and walked into the lobby.

"Perfect," sighed Carol. "Now we're really dead—there's two of them."

"Nope," said Ava, clenching her jaw. "I have an idea."

"No, no, no, your ideas are going to land us in Italian prison!" Carol exclaimed quietly.

"Trust me," whispered Ava. "I was just a little off."

Before Carol could say anything, Ava quickly stood and whipped out another quarter. They said nothing as it sailed through the air—this time missing the men, but striking a large blue vase filled with flowers on a pedestal. The quarter struck the thin glass, shattering it, and both men dove to the floor.

Ava nodded proudly. "Bull's-eye." She had made a gunshot.

Carol's eyes flew open and Ava grabbed her wrist, pulling her up as they bolted to the luggage cart.

"Okay, not exactly as I planned...but effective, right?" asked Ava once they were hidden again.

"Ask me again if we make it out alive." Carol watched in horror as a hotel staffer scurried over to the two men and they all began looking around. The bellhop was speaking into a walkie-talkie; the girls were sure he was calling Security.

"Follow me," whispered Ava urgently. Ever so slowly, she started pushing the luggage cart to the doorway on the other side of the room, aiming for the sign that read "Stairs."

The girls weren't sure if it was the slow *squeak, squeak* as the wheels turned or the cart that magically began moving by itself, but the bellhop and the two men suddenly froze and turned toward the luggage cart.

"Ava…," said Carol slowly, getting more and more anxious as the men turned and began quickly walking toward them.

"*Now.*" Ava yanked open the door and began sprinting up the steps.

Scrambling to keep up, Carol leapt up the steps two at a time. As they ran, she looked at her best friend. "You may want to actually *tell* me your plans if you want them to work!"

"Sorry! But look, first floor!" They didn't pause for a millisecond, hurrying up the stairs.

The girls raced up the steps, using the handrails to whip them around each corner. "Fifth floor, we're almost there!" Ava cried out. She could hear the footsteps of the chasing men, pounding on the staircase below them.

In full sprint, Ava burst through the doors and whipped out the room key. They flew through the hall, passing a table with a huge bowl filled with beautifully colored glass marbles, all blue and pink. On a whim Carol smacked her hand against the bowl, flipping it over. The hallway filled with hundreds of shiny glass marbles, rolling on the carpet with dull *pings*.

Just as they rounded the corner, the girls heard loud *oooph*, *oooph*s. The bad guys landed heavily on the balls, falling over themselves.

"Nice going!" Ava said to Carol. With another burst of speed, the girls made it to their door, swiped the card, and jumped inside the room.

"Shhhh, wait," Carol whispered as she held the door shut. Sure enough, they heard the men pound past, shouting Italian to each other. While quietly locking it and pulling the chain across, Carol let out a long breath. Ava leaned her shoulder against the wall, running her fingers through her hair. They stared at each other, panting.

"I think the bad guys are falling for us!" laughed Ava.

"What?" asked Carol, bewildered. "Oh…the balls. Funny," she snorted.

The girls fist-bumped; they had made it.

10
SANTA FLORIAN DEL FUOCO

After catching their breath in their hotel room, the girls hurried over to the desk. Carol stood beside Ava as she grabbed the desk chair and knelt on top of it.

"Okay," said Ava excitedly, "let's see what all of this craziness is about."

Anticipation raced through Carol, making her hands fidget with excitement. Ava pulled the copper cylinder from her pocket. It was the length and diameter of an ink pen. The ends were sealed with what looked like red wax. Ava gently shook the tube while holding it up to her ear. *Nothing.*

"It looks like the ends are sealed with wax," offered Carol.

Ava nodded. She grabbed a paperclip from a stack of her mom's papers on the desk and straightened it. Carefully, she worked the wax out of the tube. Ava turned the cylinder over, holding her hand out beneath it in case something came out. The two held their breath. They knew, without speaking, that whatever the cylinder held, it was their best chance of finding out what to do next.

Ava tapped the open end of the cylinder on her palm. There was the slightest rattle, and then a small, brittle scroll slid into her hand.

Ava offered it to Carol, who picked it up gingerly. She spread it out between her fingers before flattening it against the desk. It was hard to read, the words scrawled in slanted cursive with blotted ink. It was also hard to read them because they were written in what looked to Carol like Latin.

"What's it say, big brain?" inquired Ava.

"I'm not sure…. I think it's written in Latin."

"There's also a map," pointed out Ava. A very roughly hand-drawn map lay below the mysterious writing.

"One second," said Carol as she retrieved her tablet from beside her bed. She opened Google Translate and typed the words *posizionare il rotolo sull'altare della luce.*

Carol's eyes narrowed. "Place…the scroll upon the Altar of Light."

"Okay…this gets weirder and weirder," moaned Ava. "Let me guess, the map is supposed to lead us to the Altar of Light?"

"I think so," said Carol, studying the map.

"I wish some divine bearded guy would just come out from the clouds, point a finger, and say, 'Hey you, go there.'"

Carol nodded. "There is a shortage of divine bearded guys, that's for sure, but…we do have the next best thing."

"A map that looks like it was drawn on an Etch A Sketch?" laughed Ava.

"Whoa, that was retro. I'm pretty sure that this is the Villa de Cathedral where we found the scroll, and if we follow this line through the city, it leads to...hmmm...."

"It leads to *hmmm*? Is that Italian?"

"Well," said Carol, thinking. "According to the map, it leads to something called the Santa Florian Del Fuoco."

"Santa Florian? Is that Santa's cousin?"

"I think Santa means saint. Give me a second," said Carol as her fingers tapped away on her tablet. "This doesn't make sense. It says Saint Florian is the patron saint of chimney sweeps and firefighters. He died in 304 AD."

"You're kidding, right? Chimney sweepers get their own saint?"

"Apparently, *del fuoco* means 'of fire.' So this is a church named after a saint, who guards chimney sweeps and firefighters."

"Maybe it's some kind of clue and we're just missing it," said Ava. "It says to place the scroll on the Altar of Light...maybe it really means Altar of Fire? I don't know.... Where is the church exactly?"

"I'll need to consult *Signore* Google Map," Carol said. After Googling, she looked at Ava with a confused expression. "I can't find anything on Google for a church or building named Santa Florian Del Fuoco."

"Okay," said Ava, pointing at the map. "What is *that* thing? It could be another landmark. It looks like a bird…or an airplane."

"Wait, maybe it's an airport," said Carol. "It has three words in Italian beneath it. Aquila di Dio."

"*Aquila*? Something to do with water…and God?" guessed Ava. "A water god? Noah? The clue is in the Ark!"

"Slow down," laughed Carol. "Okay, first of all, *aquila* has nothing to do with water; it means eagle. But, if we put it all together, the phrase translates to Eagle of God." On a whim, Carol searched "Eagle of God Florence."

"I never knew God had an eagle…," mused Ava as Carol typed. "I thought that was just an American bird."

"I found it! It's a statue. And according to our lovely hand-drawn map, the statue is directly across from the Santa Florian Del Fuoco. We just need to find that statue."

"Awesome, big brain—you're brilliant!" Ava's phone buzzed, startling her. "My mom…," blurted Ava, nodding at the phone. "She says that she's looking forward to spending the afternoon with us."

Ava quickly texted her back, letting her know that everything was awesome and that she and Carol were excited about spending the afternoon with her. She finished off with "I love you" and a half-dozen heart emojis.

"So, if my mom's going to be here soon, we've gotta get moving."

"Unfortunately, we can't just leave."

"Rossi and his mutants...?"

"Rossi and his mutants," confirmed Carol, nodding. "Plus, I don't think we've endeared ourselves to the hotel staff. The fire extinguisher, the kitchen, the vase in the lobby, the decorative bowl filled with marbles in the hallway...."

"Okay, okay. I get your point. We're probably not their favorite guests. What about one of the fire escape doors? There's one at the end of our hall."

"And, what if we open it and it sets off the alarm? They're gonna kick us out of the hotel for sure."

"Well, if we can't take the stairs and we can't take the elevator...how do you suggest we get downstairs? Teleport?"

"You actually had a brilliant plan. Two words," smiled Carol. "Fire. Escape."

"You just said that the doors for the fire escape probably have alarms."

"They probably do," laughed Carol as she grabbed her jacket. "Follow me. I've got a trick up my sleeve you're gonna love."

Ava watched as Carol slid the paper scroll into the tube and put it in her pocket. She turned to Ava and smiled. "Alrighty, let's wrap this mystery up—I'm starving."

II
FIRE

"I hate heights! You know I hate heights!"

"Just don't look down," warned Carol moments after climbing out of the window at the end of their hotel hallway. She stood on a narrow, metal, grated platform that jutted out from the side of the hotel. Despite the handrails, Ava was petrified.

Ava slowly crawled out the window and stood shaking beside her friend. She closed her eyes as a wave of vertigo washed over her. She gripped the side of the hotel as her knees buckled.

"Breathe," Carol advised in a soothing voice. "Breathe through your nose."

"I'm gonna *punch* you in the nose," hissed Ava.

Ava looked at the platform of twisted black metal. She could see the ground some sixty feet below through the grated floor of the platform. "Right now," gasped Ava, "the angry hotel staff seems like a much better option."

"Look, there is a platform between each set of stairs." Carol counted ten stairs between each platform. "Just take it one section at a time."

Ava nodded. *One set of stairs at a time.*

Carol descended slowly, watching as Ava turned and climbed down the stairs on her hands and knees like a child. She felt horrible for Ava; she could see her entire body trembling as she slowly made it down each platform.

"Okay," Carol said softly. "This is our last stop. I just need to lower this ladder down and it will take us down to the ground." Ava watched silently as Carol lowered the huge metal ladder. It was connected to a pulley system that made a screeching noise like fingernails on a chalkboard as it lowered. The ladder clunked noisily to a stop about a foot from the ground.

Carol grimaced. "Okay, Aves, we gotta hurry."

Ava nodded and carefully followed Carol down the ladder, her sneakers making a *thump* as she landed. Carol bumped her shoulder gently and smiled. "You made it!"

"I did," smiled Ava proudly, feeling the color return to her face. "But I think I may need a new pair of underwear."

"Too much information," laughed Carol. "Now seriously, we have to go!"

The girls ran along the side of the hotel, careful to take in their surroundings and make sure they weren't being followed. The map took them on a journey, through alleys and narrow roadways, twisting and turning like a serpent. Perhaps it was the triumph of getting away from the bad guys and finding the scroll, but there was a zing in the air between the two girls.

Or maybe the *zing* in the air was real! Ava suddenly screeched to a halt. "Do you smell that?"

"What is it?" asked Carol, confused.

She followed Ava's trembling finger. A street vendor was tossing a disc of dough high into the air. He was making fresh pizza. Carol felt her stomach grumble; it had been hours since their last meal.

"Pizza!" whispered Ava. "Italian pizza right in the middle of the street!"

The girls ordered two pieces of sizzling hot pepperoni pizza and then found a small wooden bench under the shade of a beautiful oak tree. The girls moaned with each delicious bite of pizza.

"Okay, change to our plans," said Ava as she wiped her mouth with the back of her hand. "You continue on to the…burning altar thing. I'll stay here and keep the pizza guy company and an eye out for the bad guys. I'll text you if I see anything suspicious."

"You're such a good friend," smiled Carol as she wiped the grease off her fingers. She studied the map and then stood up to get her bearings.

"So, how much further, fearless leader?" Ava asked.

"It actually looks like we're almost there."

"Okay, let's get going. We've gotta beat my mom back to the hotel. We're already in enough trouble."

The girls continued their trek through the city, snaking down a long, winding alley. This part of the city didn't look as friendly. Trash littered the alley, and graffiti was splashed across rows of buildings as if they were brick canvases.

Carol held up her hand, and they halted. She looked up from the map. "Here…?" she exclaimed, her voice filled with confusion.

Neither spoke for a second. Ava felt the wind rush out of her. A massive wave of disappointment enveloped Carol, and she felt herself sag. "Oh, man…." She looked at the map and pointed. "This has to be right! See, the statue of the giant eagle…it's over three hundred years old. It was supposed to be right beside the statue."

Carol jabbed her finger at the map. "See?!"

Ava looked, and sure enough, directly across the square named Santa Florian Del Fuoco was a poorly drawn eagle, but an eagle nonetheless. But what lay in front of them was a huge expanse of land, filled with rubble. No kidnapped old man, no magical protectors, and definitely *no* Altar of Light.

"One sec!" Frustrated, Ava marched up to the first person she saw, a mustachioed man tending to the tires of his bike.

"Sir, *parli inglese?*" Ava asked, doing her best not to butcher the Italian language.

He nodded, stood up, and dusted his hands off on his jeans.

"My friend and I are trying to find the Santa Florian Del Fuoco. Do you know where it's located?"

The man pulled at the end of his mustache, chuckling. Ava stared at him, confused. Maybe she'd said it wrong? She tried again. "Maybe I misspoke. I'm looking for the Santa Florian Del Fuoco." She over-enunciated each word, hoping that would help.

"Ah, little girl," he said in a thick Italian accent. "I think…."

"Wait," said Carol, interrupting him. She held out the scroll to him. "It's a map," she said. "We found it in a library book," she fibbed, not wanting to give him too much information. He took it from her, then narrowed his eyes at the drawing.

"Ahh, *povere ragazze*." He tried to contain his chuckles. "I don't know who wrote this for you, but someone has played a joke on you girls. There is no Santa Florian Del Fuoco. Saint Florian of Fire?" he laughed. "This building does not exist."

"Saint Florian did exist!" Ava insisted. "He was the patron saint of firefighters and chimney sweeps!"

"That may be," smiled the man gently, seeing the girls were truly upset. "But," he continued, "the rubble you see behind you, this was the old firehouse…. It was nearly two hundred years old, but an earthquake damaged it so badly that the city was forced to tear it down."

Ava looked at Carol incredulously. "This was a firehouse, not a church? This was all some kind of crazy joke? Are we being punked?"

Carol shook her head. "Saint of firefighters…I can't believe it."

"Well," said Ava, turning and motioning at the rubble behind her. "From the looks of the building behind us, it looks like Saint Florian called in sick…. Thank you, sir."

The man nodded and waved as he wheeled his bike away. "Good luck on your adventure."

Carol and Ava sat down on the curb of the street. The same thoughts swirled around their heads. There was no way this was all a joke. A man had been brutally kidnapped, a woman's store destroyed, men had chased them through their hotel. There was just *no way* this was an elaborate joke.

"We're missing something," Carol sighed. She looked at the map. Why would it lead them to a place that didn't actually exist?

Aggravated, Carol rolled up the map, but as she went to insert it into the cylinder, she dropped it onto the dusty road. "Great," she said, picking it up and blowing the dust off the container. She froze. The dust revealed a tiny inscription at the top!

Ava stood up and brushed off the seat of her pants. "What is it?"

"I don't know—there's something written on it." Carol turned the tube. The writing was so tiny she could barely read it.

"Let me guess," said Ava. "This end up?"

"No," said Carol, squinting. "It looks like I Corinthians 313."

"Isn't that a book from the Bible?" Ava asked.

"I think so…."

Ava was already swiping away at her phone. "First and Second Corinthians were written by someone named Paul, and are in the New Testament. What did the inscription say again?"

"There is an *I* in front of Corinthians and then 313."

"Okay…," acknowledged Ava.

"Wait, you said there was a Corinthians one and two, right?"

Ava nodded. "Yes…."

"Okay, so the *I* could be the Roman numeral for one. So it would be first Corinthians 313. The numbers after Corinthians would be the chapter and the verse. How many chapters are in First Corinthians?"

Ava's fingers quickly tapped on her phone. "Sixteen."

"So, it has to be chapter three, and the second two numbers would be verse thirteen."

"Already on it," said Ava excitedly. She looked at her phone and then looked back at Carol. She cleared her throat. "'Every man's work shall be made manifest: it shall be revealed by fire…'"

Ava looked up at her best friend. "What does *manifest* mean?"

Ava could tell that Carol's big brain wheels were turning as she began chewing on her lower lip. "*Manifest*," Carol smiled, "means to display or show something."

Carol's mind was going a mile a minute. *Every man's work shall be made manifest—because it shall be revealed by fire….*

Carol's eyes flew open. "We gotta get back to our room! We need to start a fire, stat."

12
KIDNAPPED

"Mom," Ava called out breathlessly as she locked their hotel room door behind them.

There was no reply. Ava turned to face the room, and she gasped. Carol's jaw dropped. The hotel room had been destroyed. Their suitcases had been emptied on the floor, with clothes everywhere. The pillowcases had been pulled off and thrown, mattresses askew, chairs on the ground. The contents of her mom's purse were poured onto the desk, and her mom's wallet and planner were on the floor.

"Mom?" Ava called again, but this time her voice came out as more of a whimper, and her chin trembled. Carol reached out and found her hand. Ava squeezed it tightly. "She's not here," Ava murmured, choking up. Her breath started coming out in short, panicked bursts. "Carol, they took her."

Ava let go of her friend's hand to walk through the room, looking at the mess. One of her mother's lipsticks, a pretty berry color, had been uncapped and smashed onto the floor. Ava remembered that it was her mother's favorite. She bent down to pick it up, rolling it around her fingers. That feeling of cold helplessness drained from her face, and instead, she saw red.

"Carol, they *took my mom.*"

"Ava...," Carol started but had no idea what to say. She walked over to comfort her friend, but as she came closer, she could see Ava's eyes were filled with rage.

"I swear, if they *hurt* my mom...," she bit out.

"Ava, don't think like that," pleaded Carol, looking around. This was so, so awful. "We're going to figure this out."

"We can't call the police," Ava said. "If we call them, we have no idea if it will actually be the police. For all we know, Rossi has men on the inside."

"I know," said Carol gently. "We'll...," she stopped midsentence. Ava's phone was vibrating.

"It's Mom!" As Ava pressed the phone to her ear, a heavily accented voice began to speak. "Listen and listen well," it said. Ava's blood chilled, and she looked at Carol. It wasn't her mom; it was Rossi.

"Return what is rightfully ours and we will let your mother go."

13
THE MAP'S SECRET

"Where is my mom?!" shrieked Ava. She felt Carol grab her arm, but Ava couldn't be stopped. She was on a full-blown, ticked-off rampage. "You guys have been chasing us all over Italy and now you've kidnapped my mother. Are you insane?"

"Little girl—"

"Do you not *have* mothers?!" screamed Ava.

"You will calm yourself!" commanded Rossi. "Or else—"

"Ava, we don't know what they're going to do," Carol insisted quietly, eyes huge.

Ava stared at Carol for a second. Finally, she blew out a breath and closed her eyes. Carol was right. It didn't matter how upset she was. They had to focus on getting Ava's mom back safely.

"How do I even know she's okay?" Ava asked into the phone, her voice cracking at the end. She breathed in slowly, suppressing a sob.

Ava heard a rustling noise and then her mother's voice came on. "Honey, it's me."

"Mom!" her voice broke. "Mom, are you all right? Where are you?"

"Honey, I'm okay, I promise." She sounded tired, but Ava could hear the relief in her voice. She felt it too. "We're going to get through this. Just listen to the men, and…give them what they *think* they want. Listen to them."

Rossi's voice came on the phone again. "Ava, was it?" He chuckled. Ava had never heard someone so evil. "Meet us at the Piazza Carlo Goldoni in one hour. You and your little friend will come alone. And if there are any police…well, let's just say it won't be good for your mother. No tricks, no games. Bring the scroll and the ring."

"You hurt my mom…," started Ava, white-hot tears making their way down her cheeks. Her hands shook with rage, and she swallowed hard. "You hurt her, and you'll wish you were never born."

Ava heard an annoyed sigh. "Piazza Carlo Goldoni, in one hour. No games, little girl." The call went dead, leaving Ava with nothing more than silence. She held her phone away from her face, hands still trembling. Carol gently took it from her and set it down. She put a hand on Ava's shoulder.

"Ava, I'm sorry," Carol said, her face white. She couldn't even begin to imagine how scary this was for her friend. It was scary enough *not* being Ava's mom's daughter right now. She pulled her into a hug. "I am so sorry." Carol felt a shudder make its way through Ava, and she hugged her tighter. "We're going to find a way to get her back."

"I think my mom was trying to give me a clue…," she said, pulling away, wiping her eyes with her sleeve. "She said, 'Give them what they *think* they want.' We can't just give them the map and the ring! All of this will have been for nothing!"

"We do have to give them the map and the ring," said Carol. Her eyes sparkled a little. "But, your mom may be right. Give me one second…. It's about the clue that we found on the copper tube," Carol called from the bathroom. She returned holding an iron and a miniature ironing board, meant to be placed on a tabletop. She grabbed a cup off the table, filled it with water, and then poured it into the front of the iron.

"What in the world are you doing?" asked Ava, thoroughly confused.

As she plugged in the iron and changed the temperature setting to steam, she started explaining. "At first, it didn't hit me. But think about it: Everything involving that darn tube and scroll has had to do with fire. The name of the saint, the name of the altar—and then the biblical clue from Corinthians that it will be revealed by fire. So, I kept asking myself, *what will be revealed?* Then I kept thinking of the word *manifest*—like something was hidden…."

"And then no longer hidden," whispered Ava, hope filling her face.

"Exactly," nodded Carol. "And since we can't really create a fire in our room, I thought the closest thing would be an iron."

Ava watched as Carol gently pulled the map out of the tube. She opened the map and spread it across the ironing board, and then while ever so carefully pressing the steam button, she lightly ran the iron over the entire map.

"Whoa! shouted Ava. "It's working! It's working!"

Before they knew it, their simple map that looked like a child's drawing had turned into something that even Blackbeard and his pirate fleet would approve of.

"Of course, the heat activates a chemical in the paper, making the actual map appear," Carol said.

"All of my dad's dreams of me becoming a world-class biologist…wasted," Ava shook her head.

Carol unplugged the iron and pulled out her phone, and while Ava held the map spread open, she snapped a couple of quick photos. Smiling, she slipped the phone back into her pocket. "Now, we have the real map."

Ava pressed her shoulder against her friend's shoulder. "Carol, I don't think 'big brain' does you justice."

Carol waved her away. "You have a lot on your shoulders; otherwise, you would have been all over the heat thing."

"Now, for the real Altar of Light," Carol continued. The map was quickly fading as the paper cooled. "Okay," said Carol, holding the map up to the light. Her eyes quickly searched until she came upon the words *Altar of Light* written in Italian. "Oh man!"

"You found it?!" asked Ava excitedly.

"According to this map, the altar is at a temple next to the Rennes-le-Château."

"Okay, not a problem," said Ava. "We give them the scroll, get my mom back, and we go to the right altar. They'll never know!"

"Not so easy," said Carol, shaking her head. "The Rennes-le-Château is in France, plus they asked for the ring *and* the scroll."

"Oh yeah...." The information hit Ava like a ton of bricks. Any newfound hope she had went right out the St. Regis window. Disappointed, Carol looked at the map, the paper rapidly cooling. The details disappeared little by little, just like their options. She was just about to roll up the map when Ava stopped her.

"Carol, hold the map steady for a second." Ava was holding her phone. She quickly snapped a few pictures. "Just in case."

Carol nodded. "Good idea. Sadly, none of this matters without the ring," said Carol, half to herself, "even if we find the altar."

"I know, but I have to get my mom back.... I feel horrible about the old man, I really do...but it's my mom. I...I just don't see what's so special about the darn ring. I mean if I saw it on a sidewalk somewhere, I wouldn't even bother to pick it up."

"Yeah," whispered Carol, absorbed in thought. She paced back and forth across the room. She looked back at Ava. "You're a genius!" Carol quickly unzipped her pocket, grabbing the ring. She took it over to the bed and laid it down onto the silk sheet. She took out her phone and snapped several photos of the ring from both sides before picking it back up. Carol nodded at Ava, a big grin filling her face. "What exactly did your mom tell you?"

"She said she was okay, and to give the men what they *think* they want."

"Your mom is brilliant...now I know why she's an investigative journalist. The key is *think* they want...and I think I have the answer."

"Okay...I'm all ears," said Ava excitedly.

"Do you think your mom would be extraordinarily angry if we made a small purchase from a local jeweler?"

"You're not really asking that question, are you? What do you have in mind?"

"A credit card, and your amazing skills of persuasion."

14
BAMBOOZLED

Ava followed Carol across the piazza to a jeweler's shop she had noticed near *Signora* Coppola's bookstore. Carol had filled her in on the plan during their quick journey. They paused briefly, collecting their thoughts.

They were on a mission, and there was no time to waste. Ava pushed the door open, which signaled a tinkle of a bell. As they walked in, they could see glass displays covering the walls, filled with beautiful rings, necklaces, earrings, and bracelets. There was a bench in the center of the room, and a counter. The whole place sparkled, and to top it off, it smelled lightly of lemons.

"Wow," breathed Ava. "I could live here."

"*Posso aiutarla?*" asked the man behind the counter. He leaned over it, studying the girls. Gray hair surrounded his bald scalp like a halo. Scruff covered his slightly sagging cheeks, and while they made it look like he was frowning, Carol could see laugh lines on the corners of his eyes. He wore a button-up white shirt and a black vest that hung over his belly.

"*Parli inglese?*" Carol inquired.

"*Sì,*" he said. "How can I help you girls?"

"I was wondering, are you the owner of the store?"

"Yes. I'm Nico Gabriella, and my daughter Mary runs it. Now, how can I be of service?"

"Sir...Mr. Gabriella...we really need your help," blurted Ava, who marched up to the counter. "We have a huge school project that's due the moment we get back to the United States, and we're taking off on a plane tonight. We're trying to find King Solomon's ring. You know the famous ring?"

"Oh yes...I've heard the story. It gives the one who possesses the ring magical powers."

"Yes...something like that," acknowledged Ava. "Well, I sorta fibbed. I told my teacher I knew where to find it...."

Carol interrupted: "We found a man online who was selling a map that was supposed to lead us to the ring...and well, the map turned out to be fake...."

"Imagine that," he smiled politely.

"And now, I'll be returning back, without the ring," Ava said. "I can't fail this class, sir. I figured if I showed up with a ring that resembled Solomon's ring...then my teacher would at least understand how hard I tried."

"If you could help us, you might literally be saving our lives," said Carol, pleading.

And my mom's, Ava added silently.

"A school project, hmm?"

"Yes, sir," Carol unzipped her pocket and showed him the map to help bolster their story. "And here are some pictures we found on the internet. It was the closest we could find as a historical reference to the ring."

Carol handed Mr. Gabriella her phone. "Do you think you could help us?"

He looked at the photos for a moment before shaking his head. "*Mi dispiace*, girls. I have much to do today—I'm sorry." As he turned away, Ava leaned over the counter, putting her hands on the glass.

"Sir. Please." She looked at him, eyes growing huge. "We're desperate. I can't repeat the seventh grade; I really need your help."

He hesitated, looking at her.

"Please, sir." She pulled the American Express card out of her pocket and put it on the counter. "If this isn't enough, sir, I will get more…please."

Something in Ava's voice caused Mr. Gabriella to pause. "Are you sure this is just for a school project?" he asked not suspiciously, but more fatherly.

Ava fought back the tears, desperation filling her heart. "Yes, sir," she whispered.

He tilted his head and sighed. "Okay." He gently pushed the card back to Ava. "Put your money away. I do not want you to be sad. Please," he smiled, "put your money away, *piccolo angelo*." *Little angel.*

"Oh, thank you, Mr. Gabriella," cried Ava. "Thank you."

"*Prego*," he replied. He nodded to a leather-cushioned bench. "Now, go sit, and I will be done as quickly as I can." He took Carol's phone with him, looking at the photo. He shook his head and grumbled a little as he disappeared into the back room behind the counter.

With huffs of relief, the two sat down on the bench and waited. And waited. And waited. First, fifteen minutes passed, then twenty, then twenty-five. They began shifting uncomfortably, too aware of the time. They only had twenty minutes left to get to the Piazza Carlo Goldoni.

Finally, after thirty minutes, Mr. Gabriella reappeared, holding a polished ring and smiling. Ava jolted up and hurried over to him.

"Here, *piccolo angelo*," he said, placing the ring in her palm.

Ava's mouth fell open in amazement; the ring was a perfect replica.

Mr. Gabriella chuckled at her reaction. "There you go, eh?" he said, a grin in the corner of his mouth. "And if your teacher don't like it, tell them that they can take their complaints to Nico Gabriella."

"Thank you so much!" Ava exclaimed, throwing her arms around him.

"Thank you, Mr. Gabriella!" smiled Carol.

He grinned and patted Ava's back, and then with an "ehh," he waved them out of the store. Ava glanced back to smile one more time at Mr. Gabriella before they shut the door and were off again.

"We have to hurry," Carol said, panic clear in her voice. She handed the real ring to Ava, who shoved it into her sock. The fake ring went into Carol's pocket. "We don't have much time, and we've never been there before."

"Let's go," agreed Ava, and they were off, dashing to get to the Piazza Carlo Goldoni. Ava felt like she was running faster than she ever had before as they raced to their secret meeting place. Everything could be lost if they didn't get there in time.

The girls arrived at the Piazza Carlo Goldoni, stumbling onto the stone area surrounded by larger buildings. Carol couldn't help but feel a little trapped. She looked around wildly until she spotted it: a black SUV with tinted windows was parked at the curb. The streetlight above it was conveniently broken. She bumped Ava's shoulder and nodded at the SUV. That had to be them.

Just like clockwork, Rossi climbed out of the passenger side of the vehicle, shiny Italian shoes glinting in the light. The driver, a tall, thin man, still wearing a bandage on his nose, got out and leaned against the car, watching the girls. Ava recognized him as

Rossi's partner who had chased them. She glowered at the man. He should've stayed extinguished.

Rossi strode over to the pair, and Ava and Carol could practically hear the other's heart pounding. He approached them and smiled, his bottom lip stretching until it was thin. He stopped when he was a few feet away.

"I trust that you have brought what I requested?" he asked.

Ava nodded. "We did," she answered bitterly. "Now, where's my mom?"

The man turned and snapped his fingers, and the back window of the car lowered. Ava's mom sat in the back seat. She stared at her daughter, a piece of duct tape over her mouth. Even from where they stood, Ava could see that she looked frazzled and anxious.

Ava's breath caught in her throat. "If you do anything to my mom, Rossi, you are going to be in a world of hurt."

Somehow, that grin stretched further. He looked eviler than any Disney villain she'd grown up with. A chill ran down her spine. Ava pulled out the map, keeping the copper tube hidden, and Carol pulled out the ring.

"I kept my part of the deal," hissed Ava. "Now you keep up yours."

His eyes stared at the ring. That greedy look appeared in his eyes, and he started salivating again as he did in the bookstore the day before.

"Rossi!" shouted Ava. His head snapped up. "I'm not waiting anymore. You have what you want, now give me my mom!" Her anger sparked, and she wanted to charge at the man.

"Not so fast," snapped Rossi. "We need to make sure that the scroll and ring are real."

"Look," said Carol furiously, stepping forward. "We don't care about any stupid scroll and some cheap ring. We're sorry we ever got caught up in all of this craziness. Look at us! We're twelve years old! We don't want the scroll or the ring; we just want her mom back!"

The man hesitated, thinking to himself. Ava could practically hear his thoughts from where she stood. *Maybe the girls really don't have any idea what they have.* He flicked his fingers, motioning for his partner to open the door to the vehicle. Ava's mom stumbled out and stood by the car. Another man slid out the back behind her, his hand inside his jacket.

"Mom," cried out Ava.

"Say another word, and she disappears," promised Rossi. "Now, let me take the ring and the scroll. If they are both authentic…then I'll keep my deal."

The man let Ava's mom take one step toward the girls. "Mom," whispered Ava, her eyes pleading with her to tell her what to do.

Rossi stepped forward, his hand outstretched in front of him. "Now…or I'll have my men *take* them from you. Your choice," he hissed, brushing his jacket aside to reveal the taser.

Ava stared him in the eyes, anger coursing like venom through her veins. He took the map from Ava and put it into his suit jacket. He then reached out his hand and closed it over the ring like a trap, snatching it from Carol's trembling hand. He let loose a chuckle. He held it up to the light, marveling at the ring.

He glanced at the girls. "Oh, you have no idea what you've done." Rossi snapped his fingers. Ava's mom was shoved back into the car.

"Wait," started Ava, taking a step forward. He spun on his heel quickly and began to stride away.

"Wait, no! We had a deal!" She dashed after Rossi and grabbed him by the arm. With amazing strength, he flicked her off like she was a bug. She crashed to the ground, bouncing off the gray stones of the piazza and banging her knee and elbow. She gritted her teeth and struggled to stand.

"*Mom!*" yelled Ava, jumping to her feet and running toward the SUV.

Rossi calmly climbed into the passenger side and drove away, taking her mother with him.

Ava watched as Carol also had taken off toward the SUV, tugging off her shoe in the process. With an audible shout, Carol threw her shoe at the car. It roared off, unbothered, into the night.

"Why did they take my mom?" whispered Ava, coming to a stop. "We gave them what they wanted."

"They kept her as insurance...they want to make sure the scroll and the ring are real."

"What happens when they find out it's not?" asked Ava.

"I'm guessing," paused Carol, "they are going to be very angry...and demand the real ring, or there will be consequences."

Ava's knee and elbow stung as she moved. There was a kind of uncontrollable ache in her stomach. It made her feel like the wind had been knocked out of her and she was on the verge of throwing up, all at the same time.

"What do we do?" Carol wondered aloud, hands on her hips. "It's only a matter of time before they figure out that the ring is fake. How long do you think it will take them to figure out the map?"

"They don't have the copper tube with the main clue...so chances are they won't figure out the map."

"Unless the old man that they kidnapped knows the secret of the map…. I'm sure they have ways to make him talk." Carol shuddered at the thought.

"There's only one thing we can do," said Ava. She sniffed and lifted her chin. "They are desperate to get the ring. They will do anything for the ring. They're not going to do anything to my mom as long as we have this ring."

"So…what are you thinking?"

Ava's eyes flicked to Carol's. "How well do you speak French?"

Carol's jaw dropped. "Are you serious?"

Her eyes turned steely. "Dead serious. And this time, the trade is going to be on *our* terms."

Carol smiled. "I like your moxie. Those guys are going to regret the day they met us."

15
FIRST CLASS

"Ava, the taxi's here!"

Ava appeared from the bathroom with her backpack slung over her shoulder. "Just grabbed our toothbrushes. Do we need anything else?"

"I think we're good. I have the tablet and a ton of cereal bars. We both have a change of clothes, and our phones and chargers, right?"

Ava nodded. Carol slung her backpack over her shoulder too. "Good. Let's hurry. We still need to check in and I don't know if it's different in first class."

Ava let out a laugh. "Do you think they'll put down the red carpet for us?"

Carol shrugged. "If they do, I'm calling Leonardo DiCaprio as my date."

"That's fine. He's kind of looking like an owl these days."

Carol scoffed. "Ugh, does not!"

"Does too."

"Seriously, he doesn't."

"Who?" replied Ava.

"Leonardo," replied Carol, confused.

"Who? Who?"

"Oh, I get it, funny…an owl joke," moaned Carol. "Come on."

Soon, they settled into a cab. "All right," said Carol. "We have to travel to Rennes-le-Château, which is only a thirty-minute taxi ride from the airport to *Abbeye Mont Saint-Baptiste*."

"Right. And that's where you think the Altar of Light is located?" Ava asked.

She nodded. "According to the *actual* map, it's the only place there would be an altar in the area."

Ava noticed the driver looking at them strangely in the rearview mirror, his finger thumping nervously on the steering wheel.

Something about him didn't seem right…but Ava couldn't get Carol to stop talking. She was in nonstop jabber mode.

"So," Carol droned on, "it's actually a very short flight from our airport in Florence to Perpignan, France."

"Okay," smiled Ava to Carol. "Great to know. What I'm wondering is how much further to the Florence airport."

"We're about five minutes away," the driver responded. "There's very little traffic tonight. I couldn't help but hear you were flying to France. Where is it you said you were flying into? I know

France very well. I could perhaps suggest some places you would like to visit."

Carol noticed Ava's tiny headshake. "Oh no," smiled Carol. "Thank you so much. We're meeting my parents there at the airport—they've been to France many times."

"Of course, of course," smiled the driver. The next few minutes were filled with uncomfortable silence. It felt like they would never reach the airport. Finally, the cab pulled into a circular drive, filled with cabs, vans, and people walking toward the terminal. The girls quickly clambered out of the cab, grabbing their backpacks. Ava waited, tapping her foot, as Carol paid the driver. The man thanked Carol and then drove off, his cab mixing with the traffic leaving the airport.

"Okay, so did you think the driver was acting a little suspicious?" Ava queried. "I mean, he was staring at us strangely in the mirror…and then those questions."

"I guess," mused Carol. "But truthfully…right now I find everyone suspicious."

Ava nodded. "It's like we can't trust anyone."

The fluorescent lighting in the airport made everyone look pale and sickly. *You could make a killing opening a tanning salon in here*, thought Ava. Carol glanced at her phone. They had a good hour to kill before their flight, so they decided to grab some food from a small deli named Firenze's.

While Carol checked them in for their flight, Ava grabbed a couple of sandwiches and two bottles of water. When she rejoined her friend, she noticed Carol had a huge smile on her face.

"Thanks to all of the traveling your mom has done with her Amex card, you are now looking at two first-class passengers." She showed Ava her phone listing them as seated in Row 3, seats A and B.

"You are a genius. I've never flown first class!"

Carol laughed and shut down her tablet. "It wasn't me, but I'll take the compliment."

The girls gulped down their sandwiches as they watched the crowds pass through the airport. The airport was small but incredibly busy.

"Now I know why there wasn't any traffic tonight," said Carol, motioning to the crowd. "They're all here."

"I know, right? I guess we should find our gate," said Ava as she stuffed the last bite of her sandwich in her mouth.

"Yeah," said Carol, looking around. "There should be a directory or something...."

"Right there." Ava pointed to an electronic board divided into departures and arrivals. The girls scanned the board, double checking their tickets and flight numbers.

"Gate 7," smiled Ava. "It's our lucky number."

The girls began walking toward their gate, mixing into a cluster of people that scurried about in all directions. Two armed security guards passed them, staring, their faces unsmiling. Ava could see Carol tense as they passed by. The two men stopped and conversed with one another, looking toward the girls.

"Don't turn around," Ava whispered. "Just keep walking." The girls made it to Gate 7 and quickly sat in an empty row of chairs. Carol believed that at any second she was going to feel a hand on her shoulder…but the security guards never reappeared.

"I don't know," said Carol with a worried look on her face. "We are just two kids…and we're trying to board an international flight."

Ava nodded. "Haven't you seen on the news where kids do this? Just last week a fourteen-year-old flew to Australia using his grandmother's credit card. Plus, I have a plan."

"Oh no," whispered Carol. "It doesn't include whipping a quarter at the gate attendant to distract her, does it?"

"No," laughed Ava, "but it will involve something I'm amazing at."

"You're going to annoy them into letting you on the plane?" asked Carol as she crossed her arms.

"No, I'm going to use my charm and my incredible acting skills."

"That's two things," clarified Carol.

"Carol, I'm about to adopt a family."

"What does that even mean?" asked Carol, bewildered.

"Watch and learn," said Ava confidently. "Watch...."

"I know," finished Carol, sighing, *and learn.*"

A throng of people began gathering around the boarding area as the airport staff started calling out zone numbers. Ava and Carol stood, grabbing their backpacks.

"Hang back for just a second," said Ava, watching the crowd.

"No problem!" said Carol, relieved. "On second thought...," she grabbed Ava by the shoulder, "if you get me arrested, Ava Clarke...."

"Shhh!" Ava whispered. "Just play along, and give me your backpack."

Ava found her target. An American couple looking to be in their late thirties had gathered at Zone 1, assigned to first class customers. Ava turned on her charm by complimenting the woman on her jacket and incredible taste in fashion.

"Are you involved in the fashion expo in Paris? Perhaps a model?" Ava gushed.

"Who me?" smiled the woman, putting her hand to her chest, obviously flattered.

Ava expertly eased the woman into a conversation as Carol stood by, silently watching the exchange. Slowly, craftily, Ava maneuvered the conversation. She told the couple that she and Carol were flying to meet her mother, who was an international journalist, and how Carol had slipped in the shower and broken a rib. It was a tragedy, but Ava, being an amazing friend, had become her caretaker and luggage hauler. The woman patted Carol on the shoulder gently. "You poor darling," she purred.

Carol smiled, then fake-winced from the make-believe rib pain.

"If you wouldn't mind," said Ava, "we're flying first class too. Would it be too much trouble to help me with her backpack? I need to help her into her seat, and I don't want to cause a huge commotion."

"Oh, of course not!" The woman turned to her husband. "George, help that young lady."

Carol turned on the drama, bending over slightly, stepping forward gingerly.

"George, don't just stand there. Help that poor girl!"

George shot his wife a *you gotta be kidding me* look, but then awkwardly put his arm under Carol's arm, helping her forward.

Again Ava gushed her thanks, telling them how thoughtful they were. The gate attendant called for first class to board. The woman greeted the girls' new adopted parents, and then scanned Ava and Carol's tickets, smiling and waving them through.

"Oh my gosh, that was close," Carol whispered.

Aboard the plane, George helped Ava and Carol with their luggage, looking just like a doting parent. Ava awkwardly hugged him and then snuggled into her massive, comfy-looking recliner.

They looked at each other and smiled widely. Ava let out a sigh of relief and giggled as she fastened her seatbelt. They had done it. Their plan had worked.

Carol looked over at her friend and smiled. She was glad that for the moment, Ava had something fun to distract her.

"I feel like a movie star," sighed Carol. "This is the best."

Ava suddenly sat back upright, a new kind of excitement coming over her. "I just realized what we can do with first class seats," she said.

"What?"

"Hold on, I'll show you." She turned to a flight attendant. "Sir, could we please order two Shirley Temples with lots of cherries?"

"Certainly," the man replied, dipping his head and smiling to himself, bemused.

"Might as well make it a cup on the side filled with cherries," she added. "It's for medicinal reasons. I was diagnosed with scurvy."

The man arched his eyebrow and looked at Ava quizzically, and then walked off to the front of the plane.

Carol laughed and bumped Ava with her shoulder. "I can't believe you asked for a cupful!"

"He'll be well rewarded," smiled Ava as she reached into her pocket and pulled out a shiny quarter.

16
THE ALTAR OF LIGHT

A sudden jolt awakened Ava as the plane touched down at the Perpignan airport. She sat up in the seat and shook her head, clearing the cobwebs. "Did I fall asleep?"

"You did. You were exhausted…and it was really the only way I could watch my movie without you interrupting me." Carol smiled at her friend and nudged her shoulder.

"Geez, thanks…."

Exiting the plane and airport, Ava and Carol accepted the help from the kind couple, not wanting to appear as if they had deceived them. The woman hesitated; she seemed torn about leaving two kids on the sidewalk outside the airport. But Ava told her that her mom was just running a little late—that they would be fine.

As the woman looked back once more, a sharp pain stabbed Ava's heart. She knew that look; it was the worried, concerned look of a mother whose gut tells her that something isn't right. Ava dug deep, waving and smiling to the woman, assuring her that they were fine. Reluctantly, the woman acquiesced and climbed into a waiting taxi with her husband. Ava watched the red headlights disappear in the darkness as she sped off into the night.

"Ava!"

Ava breathed in the night....

"Aves! Come on!"

Ava snapped her head around to see Carol motioning her over to a taxi. A small yellow VW bug with a black stripe around the middle was nuzzled up to the curve, its electric engine purring like a kitten.

"*Parlez-vous anglais?* Do you speak English?" asked Carol as they climbed into the cab.

"Wow, you've really been expanding the languages you're learning," whispered Ava, impressed.

"*Oui.* Where do you want to go?" the driver asked in a thick French accent.

"Abbeye Mont Saint-Baptiste, in the Rennes-le-Château area," Carol replied.

"Oh," laughed the driver.

"We have a lot of repenting to do," smiled Carol.

"I see," said the driver, still chuckling. "Sit back and relax, and I'll have you there in no time."

The girls stayed silent during the drive, each staring out the window, watching the blur of landscape pass by. Ava's mind was spinning, trying to put the pieces together. It felt strange putting their hopes in a mysterious map…and an ancient legend.

Outside the girls' window, the scenic view quickly turned mountainous, grass coating huge plains with gnarled and twisted trees hunched over like old men. Carol wished they could pull over and explore. There was so much to see here, but they needed to keep going. They had people to help.

The car finally arrived at an open area surrounded by trees. The driver stopped, motioning to a building.

"Abbeye Mont Saint-Baptiste," he declared.

"This is it?" asked Ava, staring at the church.

"In all its glory," smiled the taxi driver, sweeping his hand in front of him in a flourish.

"Thank you for driving us," Carol said to the driver as they got out. She leaned in his window as he swiped Ava's mom's Amex through a portable card reader attached to his phone.

Ava pulled out a quarter and handed it to him. "Thank you for the ride, sir. *Adios!*"

"That's Spanish," said Carol, shaking her head.

"*Merci, et bonne chance,*" said the driver distractedly, looking at the quarter in the palm of his hand.

Carol leaned in toward the driver. "I added the tip when I swiped the card," she said softly to the driver.

"Ah!" He winked knowingly at Carol and then pulled the car in reverse. Within seconds he was gone. Carol turned around to look at the abbey. Ava was already marching toward it.

This place is beyond creepy, Carol said to herself.

The stone was gray and streaked with age, strips of moss growing here and there. The gothic arches weren't as magnificent as the cathedral's, but, somehow, the abbeys were more foreboding. There was a kind of air that emanated from the abbey, one that settled on Ava's skin and gave her goosebumps. It put her teeth on edge.

"This place feels off, doesn't it?" she said to Carol, who pursed her lips in agreement.

"Kind of looks like it could collapse at any moment," acknowledged Carol.

"I guess that's part of the mystical charm."

Carol paused. Pulling out her phone, she brought up the image of the map. "This is it—the Altar of Light is supposed to be in there," she nodded toward the crumbling temple.

"Okay," whispered Ava. She walked forward and opened one of the doors, waiting for the roof to come crashing down on them. When all appeared safe, she stepped cautiously into the church. She could feel Carol right behind her. Inside wasn't much better than the outside. It seemed airier, but that feeling of strangeness was more potent inside. She just couldn't put her finger on why.

The ceiling loomed over them like an angel of lethargy, swooping and dark with arches that dissolved against the walls into darkened stained glass. The tiles on the ground were arranged in a mosaic that branched out into spirals. They were so weathered and old, though, that it was hard to tell they were a design at all. No one was inside the church but an elderly, hunched-over man who slowly swept the floor. He had a crown of white hair around his bald head, soft-looking like the tufts of feathers on a duckling. His back was hunched, with a brown cloak draped over his shoulders. He reminded the girls of the old man who'd been kidnapped.

"Think it's okay if we go up to the altar?" Carol whispered.

"I don't know," said Ava hesitantly. She looked at the old man, his back bent with age—seemingly hypnotized by the back and forth rhythm of his broom whisking across the floor like a pendulum. Ava looked at Carol. "I don't think he's gonna mind…not sure if he even knows we're here."

Carol nodded. "We didn't travel this far to stop now."

"Exactly," whispered Ava, tightening her jaw.

The girls slowly walked to the front of the church and paused before the altar. Ava stared at the simple piece of architecture. At the base, two large slabs of gray stone stood about three feet tall. A thick, rectangular stone slab lay across them.

Etched into the top of the stone was the symbol for Michael the Archangel!

Ava felt her breath catch in her chest...this had to be the Altar of Light. But how was something so simple supposed to help her find her mother?

She sat on the cool stone floor in front of the altar and began removing her sneaker and sock, where she had hidden the ring.

Sweep. Sweep. Sweep. Sweep. The sound was crisp and dry as the bristles of the broom scraped across the stone floor. Ava looked up at Carol as she removed the ring and held it in her hand. It looked so tiny... so inconsequential. Carol smiled at her friend and held out her hand. It wasn't that Ava needed help standing up...it was simply the fact that Carol wanted her to know that she was there for her. That no matter what happened, she would be there for her friend.

Ava turned and faced the altar. "Please...help me find my mother," whispered Ava, her voice barely audible.

Ava slowly stretched out her hand above the altar. She hesitated. Everything had become eerily silent. She placed the ring onto the altar and waited. Nothing happened. No bolts of lightning piercing the night sky, no magical beings...only silence.

Ava closed her eyes, battling the tears that fought to be released. Her hands clenched into fists, her body trembling, disappointment threatening to suffocate her. Carol placed her hand on her friend's shoulder, resting her head against hers.

A voice gentle yet filled with authority startled the girls. It was the old man who had been sweeping the church. "My child, what is it that you've placed upon the altar?"

Ava looked at the man, feeling foolish, feeling overwhelmed.... "It's a ring," she whispered. "I'm sorry if I offended you or the altar."

"Why would you place a ring on the most sacred of altars, my child? This altar is for spiritual gifts."

"Because the scroll told us to find the Altar of Light. I thought that maybe if I put the ring on the altar...it would help me find my mother." Ava's face sank. She closed her eyes, hot tears running down her cheek.

"So, you are the ones who found the Archangel's scroll," he said kindly.

Carol nodded. "We figured out that the map had a hidden secret."

"And once you figured it out, the map led you here, to my sanctuary," smiled the old man.

Carol nodded again. "That's right. Wait, you said *your* sanctuary? Are you a priest?"

He took a step closer to the girls. "Yes, yes I am, and this...beautiful, archaic pile of rubble is my home," he laughed.

"But the bad guys...they have the map. If they figure it out, then they'll come here. I know you are a priest and all...but these guys are evil, and they have tasers."

The priest turned and looked into Ava's eyes. "My child, evil will always try to take, to destroy...." He gently touched Ava's chin, raising her face to his eyes. "I promise you, we are here to put a stop to their madness. And, don't be so hard on yourself by giving them the map. They will have to follow it, like a moth to a flame...and it will be their doom."

Ava's bottom lip quivered. This was all too intense. "The men told me if I gave them the ring and the scroll that they would return my mother," said Ava, her voice breaking. "But they lied."

"But...you still have the ring?" asked the man, looking confused.

"It's a long, long story," replied Carol, "but yes, we still have the ring."

A look of relief passed over the old man's face. He reached into his robe and removed a small black cloth satchel. His fingers disappeared into the pouch for a moment and then reappeared. He held up a small ring. "Does your ring look like this?" he asked, holding out his hand, revealing what appeared to be the other half of Ava's ring.

Ava nodded, her eyes growing wide. "You have the other half of the ring," she whispered.

"Yes." The old man approached the altar. He made a few hand motions over his forehead and chest. Then after whispering a few words, he placed the ring onto the altar, on top of Ava's ring. As if by magic the two rings interlocked, and the hexagram symbol on the front glowed a golden red. Carol scrambled backward, Ava following her.

"No way!" gasped Ava.

"Ava!" Carol breathed, looking behind them.

Ava whirled around, her mouth falling open. A dozen men and women dressed in black had positioned themselves in a semicircle behind them. Their eyes were laser focused, their mouths pulled taut. But as the priest turned, holding out the ring for everyone to see, their serious faces transformed into astonishment.

"These two brave young ladies are the reason you have been summoned here tonight," said the old man as he moved beside the children. "For they have returned to us King Solomon's ring. However, their bravery has come at a cost." He gently rested his hand on Ava's shoulder. "This child's mother has been kidnapped, and as you know, they have also taken one of our own." Ava's face burned as she felt the attention of the group on her.

"Andrew," he said, turning to face a huge, hulking man with fiery red hair and green eyes. "Secure the abbey and then meet us below.... I'm quite sure we are already being watched. We will need to proceed with caution."

As Andrew rushed off, the priest motioned for Ava and Carol to follow him. He led them to a solid wall of stone. One by one he pushed a series of stones, and a hidden doorway appeared.

Ava looked at Carol. "It's like the bat cave! A real hidden passage!"

The girls followed the old man through a narrow stone passage, huge wooden beams arched overhead. The air smelled musty and damp, reminding Carol of her parents' basement. Rows of lights, anchored to the walls, illuminated the narrow hallway. The group came to a stop at a huge wooden door, reinforced with strips of iron. The priest fished out a set of keys from beneath his robe, and moments later the door swung open.

They followed the priest as he descended down a section of stone stairs that connected to another hallway and then to another large wooden door.

"You would need a map just to figure your way through this thing," whispered Ava.

Carol nodded. "It's amazing."

The old man paused in front of another door. "Here we are."

He unlocked the door and ushered the girls forward. Ava and Carol shook their heads…this was not what they had expected at all. The room was filled with computers, massive flat screens that took up the entire wall, and technology the girls had only seen in movies.

The priest, seeing their confused expression, laughed out loud. "What were you expecting, a bunch of Knights of the Round Table?"

"We just thought…well actually, I'm not sure what we thought, but it wasn't this," said Carol, her eyes orbiting around the room.

"I'm just so confused," whispered Ava.

"This is one of our mission control rooms. We have several like this all across the globe," explained the priest. "We are tasked with protecting and moving priceless religious artifacts all over the world."

"You do a great job of hiding this place! Not trying to be rude, but the church upstairs looks like it could collapse at any second."

"Ah, yes. Perception is everything. You perceive that this place is just another old church, one of thousands in Europe about to crumble to the ground…but this façade allows us to do the Lord's work secretly and mostly uninhibited."

"Mostly?" inquired Carol, suddenly a part of the conversation.

"Ah, clever girl. Yes." He leaned in, whispering. "There is a powerful group that would like nothing more than to use treasures like Solomon's ring for nefarious reasons."

"Evil reasons," said Carol, seeing the confused look on Ava's face.

The priest quickly walked to the front of the room. Every head turned toward him. The girls listened as he laid out a three-part plan: safely hide the ring, rescue Ava's mom, and free Nicholas, the old man whom Ava and Carol had witnessed being kidnapped.

There were very few questions. This was an elite team with centuries of experience bestowed upon them by the protectors who had come before them.

When he was finished, the priest removed his robe. Underneath, he too wore a black suit, with a black turtleneck. The girls noticed that he now moved with a commanding authority. The hunch was gone, and there was a powerful light burning in his eyes. He no longer resembled the old hunched man, sweeping the abbey. He exuded power in every movement. His eyes alighted on the girls. "Okay," he smiled, gesturing to the girls to follow him. "It's time to set a trap."

17
THE GUARDIANS OF THE RING

Ava and Carol quickly followed the priest through another set of winding passageways, finally coming to a stop in front of another stone wall. The girls waited for the priest to push the stones again. Instead, he paused while a razor-thin red light passed across his eyes. Moments later, the stone wall slid open. In the moonlight was a row of four black SUVs.

"Oh, no, no, no. What is it with these people and black SUVs?" protested Ava, stopping in her tracks.

"It's okay, Aves, I think they're the good guys." Carol linked arms with her. "I mean, c'mon. He made the ring whole again. And he took us into his way cool command room…I think we can trust them."

Ava sighed. "But just to let you know, I've seen enough black SUVs to last me a lifetime."

She continued forward and the priest quickly escorted the girls to one of the SUVs. He opened the back door and Ava and

Carol slid into the car. The priest walked around the back of the car and then climbed into the back seat with them.

"Sir," asked Carol. "Just what did Ava and I get mixed up in? Why are so many people after the scroll and the ring?"

"Why not just keep it in a safe deposit box? I hear they are extremely affordable," added Ava.

"Those are great questions. Since we have a bit of a drive, I'll fill you in on a little history. For thousands of years we have protected King Solomon's ring, and for that matter, many famous ancient relics. Not only are many of the treasures priceless, but many have magical powers that we can't even begin to understand. But one thing we do know: this power would be devastating in the hands of evildoers.

"Just like with the knights before us, Solomon's ring will be divided into two halves again, and then each half of the ring will be whisked away to a safe hiding place, to opposite sides of the globe."

Ava turned to Carol. "Did he just say we are going to opposite sides of the world?"

"I'm pretty sure he said the *ring* would be taken to opposite ends of the world." Carol hesitated. "Won't the bad guys just follow you? I mean, they've been one step ahead of us, no matter how careful we've been."

The priest smiled. "Oh, they will try. But when you've been guarding a secret for centuries, you pick up a few tricks here and there."

"And airline miles…," offered Ava.

"And airline miles," he laughed.

"Oh, and I also learned that blasting a fire extinguisher at someone full force in the face is a wonderful deterrent! And a great way to quit smoking."

"Sounds like the voice of experience," said the old man, looking admiringly at Ava.

"Let's just say that ever since we witnessed Nicholas get attacked by Rossi and friends, they have been chasing us across Italy. So, we've had to be extremely creative," smiled Carol.

"Ah yes, Rossi…he is a bit of a nasty fellow. However, it seems to me that you two have executed your evasive strategy flawlessly."

"Not really flawlessly," said Ava. "If Carol and I had done a better job, Rossi wouldn't have my mom."

"Ava," said the priest gently. "Rossi wants one thing, and that's the ring. Right now, you have something in your possession that he desperately wants. You wield all of the power right now, and he knows it."

Ava shook her head and tried to smile. She hoped that the priest was right. She hoped with all her heart.

"Carol, tell me, how did you wind up with the scroll and the ring? I was confused in the church because you said that you traded the ring and the scroll for Ava's mother…yet you still had half of the ring."

"Well, I knew that if we gave the ring to Rossi he would win. I was afraid if I gave Rossi the ring he wouldn't keep his word, and then he would have Ava's mom and Nicholas. We also knew that we couldn't trust the local police…another long story. So, I took pictures of the ring, and then Ava convinced a local jeweler to make an exact replica of the ring…that's what we gave Rossi."

"Ah, brilliant!" The old man's face filled with admiration. "And then you solved the clue, to find the map that led you here?"

Carol nodded. "We figured out the map first. Once we knew where the Altar of Light was located, we no longer needed it…so we gave that to Rossi. We followed the map to the abbey, and well, you know the rest."

A glorious smile grew on the old man's face, making the white stubble on his chin and cheeks stretch. He closed his eyes and nodded to himself. After a moment, he opened them to look at the girls, his expression filled with light. "Girls, I cannot begin to tell you the debt of gratitude we owe you."

"So you're actually them?" Ava spoke up. "The warrior priests defending Solomon's ring like in the movies?"

"There's no denying it now," the old man replied, smiling and unfolding his hands. "Though I wouldn't necessarily say 'warrior.' We are peaceful men of God carrying on a legacy in order to ensure peace in this world."

"So, who are the men who are trying to take the ring?" asked Carol.

"We believe they're a part of a covert sect of radicals, attempting to steal and use the power of Solomon's ring for evil. The ring is very powerful, but there are also many other treasures that are equally, if not more, powerful than the ring. Our task as Templars is to make sure these artifacts stay hidden, no matter what the cost."

Carol leaned forward in her seat, her eyes wide. "When you say other powerful artifacts, do you mean like the Ark of the Covenant?"

The priest smiled. "Like the Ark of the Covenant. The man you call Rossi used to be in the Italian Mafia, but now he is a part of a new, dangerous group called the New Prophets, and they will stop at nothing. Rossi is merely a marionette being controlled by his master's strings. Frighteningly, we know that we now have spies deeply entrenched in our group and...we have no idea who they are."

"Well, that's terrifying," muttered Carol, shifting in her seat. "How could spies get into a secret society like yours?"

"Our lives are simple lives...we take a small pittance for pay. Our lives are devoted to keeping these ancient treasures safe. However, groups like the New Prophets try to lure us to the dark side, promising us riches beyond belief.... I fear that greed has taken over the heart of some of those among us. That is why many times we hide pieces of religious artifacts in multiple places."

"Geez, whatever happened to normal bad guys? Like *Scooby-Doo* villains."

Carol nodded. "No kidding." She looked back at the priest, narrowing her eyes. "So, you *are* a Templar?"

"Yes, we are called the Templars," the priest said, a glint of pride entering his eyes. "Perhaps I can tell you more later. But...," he looked out the tinted window of the SUV, "I'm afraid we're almost to the Porte De Brasilia."

"Whoa, whoa, wait a second—we're driving to Brazil?" asked Ava, sitting up straight in her seat. "No way would my mom be okay with *that*. Have you seen the bikinis they wear?"

"No, no, no," laughed the old man. "We are going to the coast. The Porte De Brasilia is right here in France, about...ten minutes away."

"Oh, thank goodness," Ava sighed as she leaned back in her seat. "I know that you guys have been hiding things for hundreds of years, but do you really think a caravan of black SUVs is discreet?"

The priest smiled. "Point well taken. However, soon enough, you'll realize there is a *very* good reason why we are all driving the same vehicle and why we are all dressed the same."

"I'm still confused. Rossi has my mom and he wants the ring. How is sending it off to opposite ends of the globe going to help me get my mother back?"

"I know it seems confusing, but we have set up an elaborate trap for Rossi and his men." He motioned for the girls to lean in, then whispered so no one, not even the driver, could hear him. "Remember how I told you that there are spies amongst us?"

The girls nodded silently.

"You are going to have to trust me, okay?"

Again the girls nodded silently.

"Also," said the priest, speaking out loud again. "I know for a fact that your mother is here."

Ava felt her heart leap. She narrowed her eyes. "How do you know that?"

"Because shortly after your plane arrived, a private jet arrived from Italy. I know that the jet was met on the runway by…it sounds ridiculous now…a black SUV."

"They have their own jet?" asked Carol.

"Yes," smiled the old man. "They have a great deal of resources at their disposal. My contact at the airport informed me of their arrival. He also just sent me a photo from a surveillance camera from the airport." He handed his phone to Ava. "This is your mother, no?"

Ava's heartbeat quickened as she stared at the grainy photo. It was her mother! She was here, in France! "Yes!" she exclaimed. "That's my mom."

The priest leaned forward, speaking rapidly in French to the driver. The driver nodded and flicked off his headlights. He whipped the wheel to the right, tearing off the main road onto a small gravel road. Up ahead was a taxi, hidden in the shadows.

"Wait, what's going on?!" asked Carol.

The old man leaned forward in his seat. "Girls, listen! We have but seconds! There has been a change in plans."

Carol and Ava looked at each other wildly. What was happening?

"Listen," said the old man, his voice filled with urgency, "to rescue your mom and ensure her safety, we must work quickly! Here's what we have to do. Listen carefully—it's our only chance!"

Seconds later, the girls bolted from the car, racing to the taxi, hoping they had made the right decision to trust the old man.

18

THE CHASE

Ava and Carol jumped into the back of the taxi, which instantly lurched forward, slamming them hard against the back seat.

"Buckle up, girls, it's going to be a bumpy ride." Carol tried to figure out his accent, but it was one she had never heard before.

Ava pulled out her phone. Pulling up her calls, she zeroed in on her mom's phone number. The phone rang three times, and then the voice she instantly recognized and despised answered.

"*Pronto!*"

"Listen," said Ava, her voice shaking with emotion. "I have what you want," she said lying, "and you have my mom. The stupid map sent me to some crazy priest, who only wants the ring for himself."

"Where are you?" asked Rossi suspiciously.

"We are in a cab heading for Porte De Brasilia to go back to Italy. The priest and his clone army were trying to follow us, but our taxi driver lost them."

"Do you have the ring? The *real* ring?" he hissed, his voice full of venom.

154

"Yes, I have my half. The old priest and his men have the other half. He tried to trick us into giving him the ring, but I'm done playing games. You two can fight it out. I'm done with your ridiculous hocus-pocus battle. I just want my mom," said Ava firmly.

"You know all about playing games. I have your mother—this is your *last chance*."

"Aves, please be careful. You don't...."

Ava's breath rushed out of her when she heard her mom's voice.

"Mom, it's okay!" cried out Ava. "I'm giving them the ring. This will all be over!"

Ava could hear Rossi's breath on the phone; she could tell his wheels were turning. Right now, she would do whatever she could do to get her mom back.

"Do we have a deal?!" Ava asked while gritting her teeth. "If so, meet us at the Porte De Brasilia boathouse. We're four minutes away."

Ava didn't wait for an answer. Her hands were shaking so much, the phone fell from her fingers to the floorboard. Carol pulled Ava against her. "You did great," she said, hugging her friend. "You did great."

"Thanks," whispered Ava, trembling, her voice barely audible.

The girls looked through the taxi's windows into the night. The Templars' black SUVs had vanished as if it were a dream. From the back seat they could see the driver's flat gray hat perched on top of a mass of curly hair. The driver's reflection in the windshield showed bushy eyebrows and a mustache.... Was he a Templar too?

The tiny car bounced and rocked as the driver took curves on the narrow road at breakneck speed. Carol and Ava found themselves smacked together and then suddenly slammed against the opposite side of the car.

"Precious cargo back here!" shouted Carol

"Sorry!" shouted the man back to them. "We must hurry!"

"It won't matter if we all die," yelled Carol, as the car narrowly avoided a large outcrop of rock. Suddenly, the car roared onto a paved road. Before them, they could see the ocean. Above them, the sky glittered. The taxi slowed; they were approaching the Porte De Brasilia boathouse. A black SUV was parked along the side of the road.

Ava looked at Carol. "Here we go," she whispered.

The taxi cautiously pulled alongside the black SUV, its engine still running. With a hiss, the SUV's window lowered. Rossi peered out at the girls, smiling evilly. He turned his head and spoke to the driver, who lowered the rear window.

Inside, Ava could see her mom. Their eyes met and a surge of anger flushed through Ava's body. Her mom smiled at her…the kind of smile that says, *I'm okay. Be careful. I love you!*

The taxi backed away to the front of the SUV and stopped. "Okay," said the driver, nodding to the girls. "Good luck!"

Ava opened the door and both girls slid out. The wind whipped off the ocean. Ava sucked in the salty air, trying to clear her mind. Carol moved close to Ava, her shoulder pressed against her, silently letting her friend know she was there for her.

Rossi, along with his partner whom the girls had nicknamed "The Nose," climbed out of the car.

Ava reached into her pocket and pulled out a small black box. Rossi's eyes greedily followed her hands, his mouth stretched into a wide grin.

Rossi took a step toward the girls. "I only have one thing to say to you…."

"Whatever," said Ava. stealing away his moment of power. "I get my mom, and you get the ring. Then you *leave us alone!*"

Like déjà vu, Rossi snapped his fingers and his cohort opened the side door. The Nose forcefully pulled Ava's mom from the vehicle. He stood grinning like a Cheshire cat, holding her arm tightly.

Ava's heart leapt to her throat. She needed to focus and keep her wits about her. Now was *not* the time to get sloppy.

Rossi, apparently happy with how things were going, turned back and sneered at the girls. "Satisfied with the merchandise?" he hissed, laughing at his own joke.

"Mom!" Ava cried out, her voice breaking. "Are you okay?"

"Yes, yes—Ava, be careful!"

Ava nodded and took a step toward Rossi. Something was wrong. The priest had promised he would be here, with the Templars!

"The ring," demanded Rossi, walking toward Ava.

Then Ava saw it. Behind Rossi, two quick flashes of light burst through the darkness. They were here! The Templars were here!

"Here!" she growled. "Now give me my mom."

Ava opened the box containing another fake ring, drawing Rossi closer, and just as he reached for the box, she threw it to the ground. *Whoosh!* A thick cloud of smoke erupted, engulfing Rossi and the bad guys.

"What?!" he screamed, stumbling backward and coughing, clawing at his eyes.

Suddenly a throng of people dressed in black outfits, covered from head to toe, surrounded Rossi's SUV. He spun around, confusion filling his face. "What? What is this?!" he screamed.

In the confusion, Ava's mom saw her chance to escape, throwing an elbow into The Nose's face. "My nose!" he screamed as she slammed the heel of her shoe into the instep of his foot. He fell against the SUV, screaming, his hands covering his nose.

She bolted toward Ava but was grabbed by one of the Templars. "This way!" he yelled. "This way!"

"Ava be careful!" yelled Ava's mom.

Ava watched as the two Templars quickly led her to an SUV guarded by another Templar. "We'll get the girls—you'll be safe here!" said one of the men as he slammed the car door behind her.

The Templars closed in, forming a tight circle around Rossi and his men. Rossi looked at Ava and Carol, hatred filling his eyes. "Clever girls!" he spat. "You'll regret this!"

One of the figures dressed in black stepped forward, shouting out orders. The girls recognized his voice as the priest's! The priest turned to Rossi. "You should know by now that evil will never triumph over good." He snapped his fingers and three Templars rushed forward, grabbing Rossi and his minions. "Secure them!" the priest ordered.

Rossi's head hung as two men grabbed him and began marching him to another black SUV. The Nose surrendered immediately, allowing himself to be escorted to the waiting SUV; he wasn't about to put up a fight.

The remaining Templars encircled the priest. He gave each of them an identical black box. No one knew if the box they held actually contained a real half of King Solomon's ring or a fake. Only the priest knew the contents of each of the boxes. Once the boxes had been handed out, he spoke only one word. "Go!"

The priest's plan was working perfectly! The Templars raced toward the dock, where a series of black Jet Skis, moored along the dock, waited for them. Each Templar would ride a Jet Ski out to a separate seaplane, deliver their black box, and then the seaplane would take off toward opposite ends of the globe. The ring would once again vanish into the unknown.

Ava began sprinting to the SUV to see her mom. They had done it! They had captured Rossi and freed her mom, and the ring was about to be hidden away for good!

But then…a scream tore through the night, causing Ava's feet to skid to a stop. She whirled around. *What?!* She couldn't believe it. Somehow Rossi had broken free!

"No!" screamed Ava as Rossi savagely kicked a man laying at his feet. Ava watched confused as another Templar turned and attacked another Templar…literally hoisting him up onto his shoulders and then slamming him against the car. The man crumbled to the ground in a tangle of arms and legs.

"No!" yelled Carol. "Ava, he's the spy the priest was talking about!"

The girls stared in disbelief as Rossi and the spy chased down the real Templars. The girls heard an electrical hiss. Rossi fired his taser, striking a Templar in the back as he raced to the ocean. The man collapsed and lay motionless on the ground. Rossi leaned down and snatched the black box from the man.

The girls watched in horror as Rossi's cohort tackled another Templar just as he was about to reach the dock. The man crashed heavily to the ground. Rossi's man leaped to his feet and kicked the man savagely in the ribs. He ripped the black box from the man's hand, laughing.

The old man's plan was falling to pieces in front of them. The other Templars continued their mission, refusing to turn back, undeterred by the chaos behind them.

Carol couldn't take it. She wasn't about to let Rossi get the ring! Setting her jaw, she raced off toward the bad guys.

"Carol!" screamed Ava, but it was too late. "I'm sorry, Mom!" she yelled, and then she bolted after her friend. Rossi and his men had messed with the wrong girls.

The remaining four Templars raced down the dock, their feet pounding on the wooden planks. One by one they climbed down onto black Jet Skis bobbing in the water. Seconds later, the Jet Skis roared to life, racing out into the ocean to the waiting seaplanes.

Rossi and the spy raced ahead as the girls gave chase. Rossi slid on the dock, his head twisting left and right. He was losing precious time looking for a Jet Ski. Carol sprinted down the dock only a couple seconds behind him. Her mind was reeling. What the heck was she going to do once she caught up to Rossi? She knew she had to do something fast—Rossi was getting away!

She heard the roar of the Jet Ski come to life. She reached the edge of the dock just in time to see Rossi untie the mooring rope. Rossi looked up at her and laughed. "You're too late, as usual." He pulled back on the throttle. *"Arrivederci!"* he cried, Italian for bye-bye.

"*Arrivederci* to you too, pizza face!" Carol replied. With a powerful backhand swing that would have made Serena Williams proud, she nailed him square in the chest with a boat oar she found on the dock. The impact flung him backwards into the water.

Carol clambered down the ladder, oar in hand, and jumped onto the Jet Ski. She hoped it was like her moped. She pulled back on the throttle and it roared to life, shooting her forward along the dock.

Ava raced down the dock in chase of Rossi's minion, who had commandeered another Jet Ski. In the distance, she could hear powerful engines coming to life. The seaplanes! Some of the Templars had made it!

The Mystery of Solomon's Ring

Ava looked around desperately for a way to stop the spy before he disappeared out to sea with one of the black boxes. She spotted a large fishing net wrapped around one of the dock's huge support poles. She struggled to free the net, which seemed to catch on every splinter and chunk of wood. Finally pulling it free, she ran to the edge of the dock and threw it on top of the man.

Disappointingly it seemed to have little effect...the man, covered in the net, gunned his engine and took off from the dock, looking like a bug trying to escape a spider web. Ava watched helplessly as the man had just about freed himself from the net. He was getting away!

She looked around frantically for a way to help. Suddenly, Carol whipped around the other end of the dock. A wall of water foamed and sprayed on either side of the Jet Ski. She leaned forward, holding the oar like a lance, as she raced toward the man.

The bad guy, suddenly seeing Carol bearing down on him, quickly tried an evasive maneuver. But like a trained knight, she nailed him in the chest with her makeshift lance. The man flew backwards off his Jet Ski, splashing into the water, still entangled in the net.

Ava didn't hesitate. She jumped into the water, swimming with strong, powerful strokes to the man's Jet Ski. "Awesome!!!" screamed Ava to Carol.

Ava jumped on the Jet Ski. Then, spinning it around, she and Carol grabbed the net, hauling their catch to the shore…and into the arms of the French police.

"Where did you guys come from?" yelled Carol.

"We'll take it from here," said the officers. They laughed at the man, who was still trying to fight his way out of the net, his face covered in muck and seaweed.

"There's another man up…never mind," laughed Carol, as she saw Rossi being escorted up the dock by two more police officers, looking like a wet cat.

"My mom!" shouted Ava. Ava raced up the shore to a small throng of people. From out of the group emerged a smiling face. "Mom!" yelled Ava, emotion filling her heart, tears pouring down her face. She ran to Ava, grabbing her, pulling her into her arms, burying her face in Ava's hair, kissing her forehead.

She reached out and pulled Carol into the hug, thanking her for taking care of Ava. Carol closed her eyes, feeling as much a part of the Clarke family as her own.

As the small trio pulled apart, Ava's mom stared deep into her daughter's eyes. She wiped a tear from her cheek with the back of her hand. "Ava Clarke," she whispered, "you are grounded until you are thirty."

"I know," smiled Ava, not caring. "I know."

As Ava and Carol walked arm and arm with Mrs. Clarke, wide smiles appeared on their faces. Tears streaked down the priest's cheeks as he helped pull a tired and disheveled old man from the back of Rossi's SUV. It was Nicholas!

The two men embraced, and as they pulled apart, the old man turned, catching Ava's eyes. A smile formed across his wrinkled face as he raised his hand and signed the words *T-H-A-N-K Y-O-U.*

It was too much for Ava to handle. Breaking free from her mom's arm, she ran over to Nicholas and threw her arms around him.

19
THE TEMPLAR'S CROSS

The girls stood in a small room in the abbey with the old priest. It was a simple room with a world map, an old desk, and a few chairs. He was once again wearing his worn brown robe and sash.

"We're so sorry we failed you," said Ava. "We had no idea Rossi and his partner would throw their boxes into the ocean if they got captured."

"I want to be happy," said Carol. "Ava's mom is safe, and Nicholas is safe, but like Ava said…in the end, we failed."

The old man smiled, a smile of warmth and pride at Ava and Carol. "Things aren't always what they seem to be. Not only did you rescue your mom and my dear friend Nicholas, but you also helped me find and catch Timothy."

"Timothy?" asked Ava.

"Yes," he sighed, "Timothy. His family has been in the Templars for over four centuries. But sadly, the lure of riches blackened his heart, and he turned against us."

"I'm sorry," said Carol. "I know how it feels to be betrayed by someone you love."

"It's a common theme in Disney movies," explained Ava.

"Thank you," he said kindly. "Now, do you girls remember what I taught you about perception?"

"Yes," said Carol. "People believe what they perceive to be true."

The old man nodded. "Exactly...even if it's not true." The girls watched confused as he pulled back his robe, removing a cloth satchel. He gently dumped out the contents into his palm, revealing Solomon's ring.

"Wait...," said Ava. "How? Okay...I am so confused right now."

The priest smiled. "I'm sure you are, what, with all of the dramatics, the Templars racing off in a huge fanfare to take the ring to the opposite ends of the earth.... It was just that. Nothing more than a huge fanfare, a production, a diversion to fool the bad guys. The New Prophets, and other nefarious groups like them, will try to track those seaplanes, and if we're lucky, it will take them a decade before they realize they've been duped."

Carol and Ava's mouths dropped open.

"You are good!" laughed Ava. "Better than the Avengers!"

The old man looked at the girls and laughed. "Ah, the Avengers, but who needs them when we have you two?"

The girls laughed. It was good to see the old man smiling, his eyes filled with light.

"This is incredibly awkward," said Carol, "but in all of the chaos and confusion, we never asked you your name."

"Ah," the old man smiled mysteriously. "I was wondering when you were going to get around to that. My name is Michael."

"Just like the Archangel," whispered Ava.

"Just like the Archangel," winked the old man affectionately.

"Seems fitting," smiled Carol.

The old man glanced at his watch and then looked down at the girls. "I have something for each of you. The Templars will forever be indebted to you, and your bravery." He reached into his cloak and removed a necklace with a solid gold medallion of the Templar's cross.

"Ava," he said, smiling affectionately, "this is for you, for your bravery and your tenacity." He gently placed the necklace around her neck. He then kissed her forehead. Ava felt her cheeks go red, a sense of pride filling her heart. "Thank you," she whispered.

"Carol." He looked into her eyes; she could feel the gratitude radiating from him. "I have something for you as well." He pulled out an identical necklace and placed it around her neck. "I give you this necklace, only worn by the Knights Templar. This is for you, for your bravery, your wisdom, and your devotion to your friends." He gently kissed her forehead.

Speechless, Carol raised her hand to her chest, feeling the golden cross.

"These necklaces will be a signal to other Templars around the world that whenever you are in need, we will be there for you."

"It's better than a car insurance commercial!"

Carol smacked Ava on the back of the head. "Respect, honor, humility…anything," said Carol, rolling her eyes.

The old man laughed, shaking his head. "Ava, I will always remember your wonderful sense of humor." Ava hugged him.

Michael led the two girls back into the sanctuary, where Ava's mother sat quietly. He spoke briefly to her while the two girls made their way to the Altar of Light. It had been a crazy journey, but they hadn't given up.

They jumped as Ava's mom's voice gently called out to them. "Girls, it's time to go." Ava and Carol each locked an arm into Mrs. Clarke's arms and slowly walked through the church. The trio turned and waved in unison to Michael as they walked out the door and into the night.

Michael laughed a wonderful laugh from within the church when he heard Ava's voice cry out, "No, not another black SUV!"

We hope that you enjoyed reading The Mystery of Solomon's Ring. Be sure to check out our other exciting books in the action-packed Ava and Carol Detective Agency series. Upcoming titles:

If you enjoyed the book, please leave a review on Amazon, Goodreads, or Barnes & Noble. We'd love to hear from you! Thank you so much for your help, we are incredibly grateful!
Learn about new book releases at avaandcarol.com

Others by Thomas Lockhaven

Others by Thomas Lockhaven

Made in United States
Orlando, FL
07 February 2022

14550026R00114